THE CAPTAIN'S WOMAN
THE THOMPSONS OF LOCUST STREET

HOLLY BUSH

Holly Bush Books

Copyright © 2022 by Holly Bush

All rights reserved.

No part of this book may be reproduced in any form or by any electronic or mechanical means, including information storage and retrieval systems, without written permission from the author, except for the use of brief quotations in a book review.

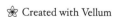 Created with Vellum

CHAPTER 1

December 1870

MUIREALL THOMPSON ROSE FROM HER DINING ROOM CHAIR IN the Thompson family home on Locust Street in Philadelphia. She'd sat at the head of that table since they'd lost their beloved parents on their family's escape across the Atlantic Ocean in 1855. She was nearly fourteen at the time, and she'd governed the family since then. She'd had help finding a home in a foreign city, furnishing it, raising her siblings, including a babe in arms—her youngest brother, Payden Thompson—from Aunt Murdoch, who was now slowing down in her old age. But her aunt was still lively, and more importantly, she was Muireall's last connection to the prior generations of Thompsons. To Scotland. To their family's place in society and the world of the nobility.

Aunt Murdoch sat at the other end of their large dining table, surrounded by Muireall's siblings and the spouses of those who were married. There was even a wee nephew napping in a crib upstairs and a child on the way for her brother James and his wife. But now there was a commotion in the hallway, where their housekeeper's son had gone to answer the door. Muireall heard shouting and a masculine voice calling the name of the young child sitting at their table, now scrambling to get down from her chair.

"Ann! Ann! Are you here?" the man shouted. "Ann!"

"Papa! I am here, Papa!" the girl said as she wiggled out of her seat. She flew into the man's arms as he came through the dining room doorway, dropping his cane as he bent towards her.

"My girl! The nuns said you'd gone with someone, and I didn't know who that person was. You must never do that again," he said, holding her tight and kissing her face and hair.

Muireall looked at the man, clearly the child's father. "The Sisters of Charity would have never allowed a child to be taken by a stranger, sir. They've known me for years."

"But I don't know you, and my Ann is most precious. I can't countenance her wandering off with strangers."

"I have just explained to you that I am well-known at the orphanage. Ann had not eaten all day, thinking you were to return for her and that you would eat together. Should I have let this dear child starve because you were late returning? I think not," Muireall said, her voice rising. "Instead, I brought her home to dine with my family."

The man looked away, turning his hat in his hand. "I was to be back from this appointment by midafternoon, but the man I was to speak to did not return until an hour ago."

"What appointment could possibly be so important that you would worry a hungry child?" Muireall replied. She could feel anger welling up in her throat. The nerve of this person to come into her home and accuse *her*!

"I was seeing this man about work, ma'am. Work I need to make sure Ann has food on the table and clothes on her back," he said, *his* voice rising with each word.

"Papa! The stew is delicious, and there is butter for the rolls! You may have mine, for I'm sure you have not eaten."

Muireall's brother stood, glancing from her to the stranger, smiled, and put out his hand. "James Thompson. Won't you join us for a meal?"

"Captain Anthony Marcus of the Forty-Second. Excuse me. No longer captain. Just Anthony Marcus now. It's a pleasure to meet you, sir."

"That's my sister you're arguing with, *Miss* Muireall Thompson."

Muireall glanced at James. What was he about? she wondered. He scooted Ann's chair closer to him and instructed Robbie to bring a chair for the captain. No, not the captain. Just plain old Anthony Marcus. What a way to introduce yourself to a room full of strangers whom you've just interrupted during their evening meal!

The housekeeper hurried to Mr. Marcus with a plate, silverware, and a napkin. He pulled his chair in and looked up at Mrs. McClintok. "Thank you, ma'am," he said as he took the glass of water from her hand.

"Captain? We're having beef stew. Allow me to dip you some," her middle sister, Elspeth, said.

"Pass the rolls to the captain," her youngest sister, Kirsty, said to her husband.

They were all smiling at the man as if he had not disturbed them and insinuated himself into their own family meal. Although, she would admit that was hardly fair. James had been the one to ask him to stay—and with that mischievous glint in his eye that Muireall did not trust.

"Thank you, ladies," he said, nodded to her sisters, and spread his napkin on his lap.

"There is butter for the rolls, Papa," Ann whispered. "Mr. Thompson will help you butter it. He helped me."

"That was very kind of him," Mr. Marcus said. But Muireall could tell Ann's excitement over buttered rolls was embarrassing to him even as he watched her bite her roll and lick the extra butter from her lips.

"There is wine, Captain, or whiskey, if you'd prefer," Elspeth's husband, Alexander Pendergast, said and lifted the bottle.

"Whiskey would be welcome, sir."

"What s-sort of work was the man offering?" Dr. Albert Watson, Kirsty's husband, asked.

Muireall watched as her family prodded him with more gentle questions. Soon he was comfortable and responding to everyone, even eliciting a laugh from Aunt Murdoch. Muireall was so angry she was having difficulty eating her meal. She'd smashed her fork into the potatoes with exaggerated strength, making her stew into a mashed mess with a few pieces of beef dotting it.

And what, after all, was she so angry about? A lonely child? A hungry one? The implication that she'd somehow spirited Ann away for some terrible purpose? Instead, she'd just brought the child here to enjoy the warmth of her home—her dress and stockings were thin—and to have a filling meal. She looked up when she heard her name.

"Are you finished?" Elspeth asked softly, holding several empty bowls in front of her.

Muireall realized she'd missed several minutes of the conversation and that she was no longer hungry. She handed her dish to her sister at the same time Mr. Marcus stood.

"I thank you for your hospitality," he said and turned to Muireall. "And for your kindness to Ann. She has enjoyed herself immensely."

"Won't you stay for dessert?"

"Or coffee?"

"I've made bread pudding," Mrs. McClintok said from the doorway to the kitchen.

He shook his head, stubborn man. "Come along, Ann."

"I've never had bread pudding, Papa. What does it taste like?"

"We will try it another time. Where is your coat?"

"But, Papa . . ."

"Ann. Please thank Miss Thompson. We do not want to overstay our welcome."

Ann Marcus daintily wiped her mouth and climbed down from her chair. She squeezed past her father, stopped at Muireall, and put her hands up. Muireall shoved back her chair, her vision swimming before her. She swiftly picked up the girl and hugged her tightly. Little arms wrapped around her neck.

Ann whispered in Muireall's ear, "I am so glad you brought me here and that my Papa got a full meal. He is always hungry, I think."

"It was wonderful having you here, Ann. Perhaps we will see each other again at the orphanage."

"Oh, I hope so. I do hope so," she said and slid down to stand. She turned to her father. "I'm ready, Papa."

They walked to the foyer, and Muireall helped Ann put on her coat, pulling the collar tight and buttoning it to the top. He stood at the door still as a stone, staring at her as she straightened.

"I'm afraid I owe you an apology, Miss Thompson. I was worried about Ann but should have never implied that you or the sisters would have anything but her best interest in mind."

Muireall looked up at him. He was a handsome man, if a bit gaunt, with firm lips and a straight nose. She could see the shadow of his beard just beginning. He was leaning heavily on his cane. "I can understand your panic, sir. Ann is a dear girl, and the two of you are clearly very close. I could have left a note for you with the sisters."

Mrs. McClintok bustled into the foyer and handed Mr. Marcus a bag. "There is some bread pudding and syrup for on top in a tin for Ann."

"Thank you, ma'am."

Muireall continued to stare at him as he watched Mrs. McClintok hurry back down the hallway. He was a compelling figure in addition to being attractive in his looks. There was a command about him, even as she sensed he was skimming very close to the bottom of desperate circumstances. The nuns had said he was a widower and that he brought Ann to them often while he searched for work. It surprised her that she'd not seen the girl before today. Muireall opened the door behind her to a rush of cold air and whirling snow.

"Oh my goodness," she said and quickly closed the door. "I didn't realize it was snowing. Have you a horse or a carriage?"

He shook his head and bent down. "We will be fine. Ann, climb on my back and hold tight."

"Oh no. Oh, please don't take her out in this weather, sir." Muireall busied herself pulling the child's dress and coat around her legs, which had ridden up when she climbed on her father's back. "How far must you go?"

"Devlin Street, ma'am. We are accustomed to harsh weather, aren't we, Ann? We will sing our songs and make the time hurry by."

"Devlin Street?" James said as he came into the hallway. "That's ten blocks away at least. My carriage will be here any moment. Let me take you both home."

"I won't put you to the trouble, Mr. Thompson," he said.

"I wouldn't have offered if I minded. My wife would have my hide if I let you walk in this weather," James said and turned to Muireall. "I didn't even realize it was snowing."

"There's no coal left in our room, Papa. Remember, I told you this morning."

"I will go back out and fetch coal once we are there. Mrs. Phillips will let you sit with her while I'm gone."

"Yes, Papa."

Muireall looked from Mr. Marcus to Ann, who's eyes were filled with tears. "Mr. Marcus, may I speak to you a moment?"

Elspeth materialized in the entranceway and plucked Ann from her father's back. "Let me show you something in the sitting room, dear."

Muireall waited until the door closed behind Elspeth and James wandered down the hallway. She looked up at Mr. Marcus, seeing he was quickly losing patience or dignity or whatever caused proud men to fume. "Please allow Ann to stay the night. I will bring her to the orphanage tomorrow morning first thing. My brother or one of my brothers-in-law will see that I have a carriage to do so. I don't believe Devlin Street is far from the orphanage. Please, Mr. Marcus. I just don't want that child to be cold."

"And you think I wish her to be cold?" he growled.

"Of course not. But sometimes circumstances require us to accept assistance. James's carriage will be here any moment to take you to your room, but Ann said there is—"

"There is no coal, Miss Thompson." He glanced around the foyer and took a deep breath. "I would be indebted if you would keep Ann here until tomorrow."

MISS MUIREALL THOMPSON WENT FROM BEING A RATHER stern and serious woman, unassuming in her looks, to one of beauty so startling that when she smiled, as she was doing now, he could barely draw breath. The transformation was astonishing. He turned quickly away from her and went into the sitting room in search of Ann. If she was not comfortable staying, he would carry her in his arms to their rooms if it took him all night.

"Ann?"

"Yes, Papa," she said and hurried to him.

"Miss Thompson has offered to allow you to stay tonight so that you do not have to venture out in this weather. But if you would rather not—"

"Yes. Oh yes, please." She reached her arms to be picked up, and he complied. "But will you be all right? I will be worried about you."

He chuckled. "I'll be fine. I weathered through colder nights than this during the war."

"But you were younger then," she said. "Just please remember to get yourself coal and take the pudding with you, Papa."

"I *was* a younger man, but I will endeavor to stay safe." He smiled at her. "Now, give your Papa a kiss."

Anthony refused the offer of a carriage ride made again by Mr. Thompson, the brother who'd asked them him to stay for a meal. He went slowly down the three wide steps in the front of the house and pulled his collar tight, careful not to put too much weight on his bad leg.

He carried the sack with the pudding and syrup after Ann insisted he take it, to his further embarrassment. The Thompsons would think he was some poor soul unable to care for his child, a cripple, rubbed down to a nub, with no coal for the stove. He laughed grimly as he turned the corner on the next block, heading toward Devlin Street. He *was* rubbed down to a nub, and his very meager savings had dwindled to a few dollars. He had next month's rent but would have to have an income for the following month if he was to keep a roof over Ann's head. His jaw clenched, and his stomach roiled with that thought. He'd seen the homeless in the city, the children dressed in rags against the bitter Philadelphia winters sometimes alone on the street while the mother or father worked piecemeal on the docks—or for the women, a much worse occupation.

He could live on the street if he had to, and he was sure the sisters would take Ann into the orphanage, but separating from her, not hearing her lively chatter or seeing her smiling eyes would certainly be the death of him. He hoped after today's interview he would be employed, even though the work was well beneath his capabilities and Mr. Endernoff seemed like a pompous ass, eyeing Anthony's faded coat and missing gloves. But he was thankful regardless. The snow made walking treacherous, but he was alive, on his feet, even if one foot wasn't as whole as the other, with a full belly, pudding in his pocket, and Ann getting the spoiling of her life, undoubtedly. He smiled. She'd taken a liking to Muireall Thompson, he could tell, and she to Ann. What an incongruous pair, his cheerful daughter and a woman who looked as if she had the weight of the world on her shoulders.

CHAPTER 2

Payden carried Ann upstairs after playing several games of checkers with her, the two of them stretched out on the floor in front of the fireplace. Muireall had read aloud to her from a book of fairy tales earlier in the evening and was impressed with her ability as she read along, though the child claimed she was not enrolled at a school, even the small one associated with St. Vincent's church, the orphanage's sponsor.

Muireall followed behind them up the steps, thinking about the cold Mr. Marcus must have faced on his walk home. It was surely not good for his injury or whatever caused him to use a cane.

"Put her in Elspeth's old room," she said as her youngest brother glanced at her. She'd already come up to the room, checked the fire, and run the bedwarmer between the sheets. She'd even found a small flannel nightgown at the bottom of one of the dresser drawers. Muireall had held it up, thinking she could cut off much of the bottom and re-hem the ruffled edge to fit the child but had dropped her hands instead. Ann Marcus would not be staying over again. The thought made her inexorably sad. She would have liked to have children, but it was far too late now.

She looked at the nightgown in her hand again. But perhaps a heavy chemise or petticoat could be made of it to guard against the winter winds. It could be stitched in the morning in little time.

The child's eyes fluttered open, and she kissed Payden's cheek. "Thank you for carrying me up, Mr. Thompson. I am so awfully tired."

Payden sat her on the edge of the bed. "Just Payden," he said.

Muireall knelt down and unhooked the long row of buttons on the girl's shoes. She began to pull her dress and petticoat over her head, but the child resisted.

"I sleep in my dress, Miss Thompson. It is warmer that way."

Muireall smiled. "Well, for tonight I have a nice, warm nightgown for you to wear."

"Oh," the child said, looking at the gown Muireall held. "It is very pretty."

Muireall helped her change clothes, wiped her face with a warm towel, and brushed her long, thick hair. Ann could barely hold her head up as Muireall braided it. She tucked her into the bed, sat down beside her and laid her palm on the child's cheek.

"It is so lovely and warm in this bed," Ann said, gazing up at her. "Will you sit here until I fall asleep?"

"Of course I will." Muireall bent down and kissed her forehead, closing her eyes to the sudden lurch in her heart.

Ann was asleep in moments, but Muireall stayed for ten minutes or more, making sure she slept soundly. She finally stood, picking up the discarded dress, petticoat, stockings, and shoes and quietly closing the door.

MUIREALL SAT BESIDE ANN WHILE SHE ATE HER BOWL OF oatmeal and several slices of thick bacon the next morning.

"Thank you very much, Mrs. McClintok. This was delicious, especially with sugar and cinnamon on top!" She giggled and turned to Muireall. "May I take this last slice of bacon with me for later?"

"I've got a bag packed for you and your father's luncheon," Mrs. McClintok said.

"Oh," she said and blushed. "Papa may not eat any of it, but I thank you anyway."

"A stubborn one is your Papa?" the housekeeper said with a smile.

Ann frowned. "Not stubborn, but . . . well, maybe a bit stubborn. But still the best Papa in the world!"

"I'm sure he is, little one," Mrs. McClintok said.

"Come along now, Ann," Muireall said as she stood. "I hear my brother's carriage out front."

Muireall helped her with her coat, which Mrs. McClintok had brushed the night before, and wrapped a scarf around her neck.

"This matches my coat!" She smiled. But the smile soon faded. "Papa says we should not accept charity of things that some poorer soul could use more than us."

"I make five of those a month in the winter for the sisters to hand out. They can do with four this month. Wrap it around your neck, child," Aunt Murdoch said from the door of the sitting room.

"It is so soft!"

"Of course it is. Miss Thompson's sister owns a store that sells Scottish yarn and fabric. The best wools you'll ever find. She gives me as much yarn as I can knit, so don't let your Papa make a fuss. Tell him Aunt Murdoch insists. And anyway, I'm making you matching mittens, so you must keep the scarf."

"Oh! That would be so nice!"

Mrs. McClintok hurried down the hall carrying a large canvas bag. "Here is something for your noon meal. It is heavy. Let Miss Thompson carry it for you."

Ann and Muireall hurried to the waiting carriage, where James's gruff coachman, Bauer, held open the door. He was an ex-boxer, too old to fight and down on his luck with an ailing son to care for, who'd taken to standing outside the Thompson Gymnasium and Athletic Studio. It had been built with Elspeth's husband's Pendergast money and was very successful because of James's management and the Thompson name, synonymous with his championship boxing.

James had put the out-of-work boxer to work as his coachman, and he'd proven to be fiercely loyal, willing to battle anyone who threatened James, but more importantly anyone who threatened James's wife or sisters. Muireall thought he looked wildly out of place in his expensive dark gray uniform and cape, as his nose laid nearly flat against his face, a patch covered his missing left eye, and his face showed his typical gruff countenance.

"How is your son, Mr. Bauer?" she asked as he held the door of the carriage and took the canvas bag from her hands.

"Doing a mite better since Dr. Watson come to see him, ma'am."

"That's very good, Mr. Bauer. I am so very glad to hear it. I've got several pairs of pants and a few shirts that no longer fit my youngest brother that I think may suit your son. I'll make sure they are sent to you."

"That's right kind of you, ma'am. Let me help this little child," he said and lifted Ann off her feet and into the carriage. "You're light as a feather, miss."

Ann smiled up at the man. "Oh no. My Papa said I weigh seven stone, but I don't believe him."

Bauer huffed a laugh. "Did he now? You tell him that Mr. Bauer, *James Thompson's* coachman, begs to differ."

Ann giggled. "I'll be sure to tell him."

Muireall realized this child had a real gift for bringing joy to her fellow man. She was guileless and seemingly unafraid even of a man such as Mr. Bauer, who did look intimidating and rough. But there he was smiling at her as he turned his hat in his hand. Muireall put her own foot on the carriage step, and he turned quickly to help her inside. She saw him check the door latch and walk around the back of the carriage, hollering up at the young man riding there to keep his eyes looking about for any trouble. He walked around to the other side, checked that door, and then she felt the carriage dip as he climbed up.

"The seats are very comfortable, are they not, Miss Thompson?"

"Very. Mr. Thompson's wife is accustomed to very fine things, and my brother indulges her at every opportunity."

"How very generous," Ann said softly and looked out the window.

It was not long until the carriage pulled up at the orphanage. Mr. Marcus himself was waiting there and opened the door. Ann flew into his arms, and he hugged her to him.

"My darling girl. I missed you," he said.

"I missed you too, Papa, and I have so much to tell you." She said pushed herself down to stand on the snowy stone walkway in front of the orphanage and turned to Muireall. "Thank you so much for allowing me to stay with you. It was great fun."

Muireall knelt down, and Ann rushed forward to be embraced. "I can't remember when I've enjoyed myself quite so much, dear."

It was a solitary moment for Muireall, even holding Ann in her arms and kissing the child's hair. There was something defining about the emptiness she felt when her arms closed around the child. She'd always been certain that raising her siblings, guarding her family and their connection to Scotland and its fortunes were all she ever needed or wanted. But as the child's fingers touched her neck above her cloak, she knew with clarity that she'd been fooling herself for years. She'd suspected as much as her siblings began to marry and begin families of their own, families of which she was on the periphery rather than at the center. And she knew there was something missing in her life. Something tangible and genuine that went to the heart of her. She closed her eyes for a brief moment to regain her composure.

Ann pulled out of her arms when the door to the orphanage opened and young Sister Ann Marie called to her to come in out of the cold. Muireall stood and faced Mr. Marcus.

"I hope she was not too much trouble," he said.

"She could never be trouble, sir. Never," she said with more emphasis than was necessary.

He stood military straight, feet spread although listing to his side with the cane, his free arm folded behind his back. "I am very grateful for her to have someone fuss over her, especially . . . a woman. She misses that, I believe."

"You're a widower?"

"I am. My wife left us and died in a carriage accident not long after. My sister came around and always made much of Ann when we lived in New York, but she remarried and moved south with her new family."

"So it is just you and Ann."

"Yes."

"I'm sorry about your wife's death, Mr. Marcus."

"Don't be," he said gruffly. "She's not deserving of it."

"I see."

"I doubt that you can, Miss Thompson," he said with an unfriendly smile. "I highly doubt it."

Muireall stared at him for several uncomfortable moments before turning to the carriage. "Mrs. McClintok sent something for your and Ann's lunch. Do not give me that look, sir. She thought that since you were busy looking for work, you mayn't have time to prepare a noon meal."

"Or perhaps there's nothing in my pantry."

"Perhaps, but that is not my or Mrs. McClintok's knowledge or business."

He picked up a bag from the ground beside him, handed it to her, and took the canvas bag. "Mrs. McClintok sent coffee with cream in a jar that I warmed on the stove and had with my bread pudding. It was a treat. I'm sure Ann had some last night. I'm returning the jar."

"She did have some—two portions, in fact," she said with a trace of a smile. "She enjoyed it very much."

He chuckled then. "I'm sure she did."

Muireall turned to Mr. Bauer. "Would you please plan on picking me up around two, Mr. Bauer?"

"Yes, ma'am." He nodded, then called out to the horses and began down the street.

"I'll be taking Ann to our rooms now," Mr. Marcus said, "but she'll have to return after lunch. Mr. Endernoff, who I interviewed with yesterday, has sent a note round asking me to come to his office at one today."

"Oh, that could be good news, couldn't it? Would he call you to come see him again if he weren't offering you the job?"

"The same thought occurred to me, but I try and not let myself hope too much. It's been a long spell since I've had steady employment, and I've talked to many men about jobs they were offering, but nothing has come of it."

"You don't want to be disappointed."

He shook his head. "No, I don't. There is only so much disappointment one can take until one becomes bitter. Ann does not need her father, her only parent, to be bitter."

"She does not. She is very, very lucky to have you, though."

Muireall turned to the orphanage door, and Mr. Marcus followed.

Anthony and Ann climbed the steps to their room a short time later. She was chattering about the Thompson coachman, a gnarly looking man complete with a missing eye, who said she was light as a feather, which tickled her to no end.

"And look at this, Papa," she said when they were inside, the door closed against the cold stairwell. She lifted her dress. "It is a petticoat made of wool flannel. It is ever so warm on my legs when the wind blows."

"I'm sure it is. What have I said, though, about accepting charity? We have a roof over our heads and food on our table. There are others who need that charity more than us, Ann."

She fixed him with the stubborn stare she displayed occasionally when she was particularly upset with him. "Aunt Murdoch said I was to tell you that my new scarf is one of five she knits every month for the sisters to give out, using wool from Miss Thompson's sister's shop, and that they were only to get four this month. She is making me mittens to match and said if you were angry about it you must speak to her."

"A scarf too?"

Ann's lip trembled. "It is ever so soft and warm and matches my coat. Please, Papa. Please. May I keep them?"

Anthony dropped down onto the chair behind him, staring at her. At his precious daughter, now begging to keep a scarf. "Yes, of course, you can keep it. It was very kind of Mrs. Murdoch to make it for you."

She climbed into his lap and laid her head against his chest. "They are both new, the petticoat made this just morning. I played checkers with Miss Thompson's brother last night while Aunt Murdoch knitted this scarf," she said. She sniffed and whispered, "Am I too greedy? Shall I give them to the sisters?"

He damned his injury and his temper and kissed the top of her head. "Absolutely not. They were made for you, and you should wear them. I'll have to be looking to get some new dresses for you in the spring since you're growing so quickly."

"Thank you. I missed you last night. Miss Thompson read some fairy tales to me, but I was so sleepy."

"I missed you too, darling."

Ann climbed down from his lap and turned to him, her smile back on her face, although her eyes told a different story.

"Let's see what Mrs. McClintok packed for us for our luncheon."

NEAR ONE O'CLOCK, MUIREALL HEARD ANN'S PIPING VOICE speaking to one of the nuns, telling her about the new petticoat Muireall had made her. Ann spoke to all the nuns, addressing them and many of the children by name. Muireall was instructing several of the older children in their addition and subtraction in a small room with low tables and chairs. Ann came to stand in the doorway but did not say a word since the students were busy working on problems.

Muireall stepped out of the room and closed the door. "Has your father gone to his meeting?"

Ann nodded. "I wished him good luck and kissed both of his cheeks. I asked Sister Ann Marie to pray for him, and she did!"

"Of course she did."

"I so hope he has a good meeting," she said. She glanced away and held her hands tightly. "I worry about my papa."

Muireall knelt on one knee in front of her. "Your father would not want you to worry about him. He is a grown man and will do what is necessary for his family."

She nodded, tears shimmering in her eyes. "He tries to act as though his leg does not hurt or that he is not disappointed when he is not hired somewhere, but his leg does hurt him and he is disappointed."

"Let us think good thoughts for him, then. Let us think that he will have steady employment very soon. And hope that his leg continues to heal."

"You're so right, Miss Thompson. Papa says we must be positive in our thoughts for good things to happen," she said, a serious look on her small face. "But I will still worry about him."

"We always worry about the people we love. It is human nature to want the best for those who mean the most to us."

Ann wrapped her arms around Muireall's neck, the child's breath warm against her skin, her head nodding. "My papa means everything to me."

Ann followed her back into the classroom and worked on her sums along with the older boys and girls. Muireall was impressed with the speed she solved the problems and how readily she agreed to help another student. Muireall was fond of her, most fond, but more than that, she admired Ann, which was strange considering the girl was just eight years old. Muireall heard voices in the hall, and Ann jumped from her chair, scooting quickly through the makeshift desks. Muireall followed her out the door.

"Papa, I heard you," she said and stuttered to a stop. "Miss Thompson and I were thinking good thoughts for you, and the sisters prayed for you."

Mr. Marcus smiled at her. "They were not wasted, your thoughts and prayers."

"Oh, Papa! Have you had a good meeting, then?" she asked, her hands together at her chin.

"I have. Now come give your old papa a hug and a kiss."

ANTHONY GLANCED AT MUIREALL THOMPSON OVER ANN'S shoulder, and their eyes met and held. Ann shimmied out of his arms.

"I must go tell the sisters that their prayers worked!"

"Was it a good meeting?" Miss Thompson asked quietly.

He nodded and then shook his head. "Endernoff hired me today, but the job doesn't start for six to eight weeks. I accepted and am just hoping I can pick up enough odd jobs to pay our rent until then." He looked at her and grimaced. "Why am I telling you this?"

"Perhaps you don't have anyone else to tell at this moment in your life. And you can't tell Ann the entire story. She won't understand and will only worry."

"In the grand picture, six weeks is not very long," he said. "But eight weeks could be troublesome. I'll have to ask for an advance on pay in either case."

Miss Thompson was silent for several long minutes. She was seemingly composed, her face showing no signs of angst or concern. Her eyes told a different story, at least to him.

"You must tell me if you are unable to keep your residence. You must promise me. I will keep Ann at Locust Street until you are again in a fixed place."

"Miss Thompson . . ."

"Promise me, Mr. Marcus. I really must insist."

He smiled ruefully. "You have nothing to hold over me to insist I do anything, ma'am."

She stared at him. "Your honor, sir. I hold up your honor. You will bring Ann to me if your situation is dire."

"If I am sleeping in the street," he said, feeling anger rise in his gut, "I would never allow her to spend the night outside. She can stay with the sisters, if necessary."

"I will have your promise, Mr. Marcus. She will come to Locust Street."

He took a deep breath and nodded. He would not argue with her because he would not allow it to come to that.

CHAPTER 3

Mrs. McClintok was waiting in the foyer when Muireall walked into the Locust Street house the following week. "Mrs. Thompson is in the parlor, Miss Thompson. Here, let me take your hat and coat."

Muireall straightened her hair and went directly to the parlor to greet her brother James's wife. "Lucinda. What a lovely surprise. I see Mrs. McClintok has brought coffee."

"Tea, actually. Coffee no longer agrees with me," she said as she placed her hand on her swollen stomach.

"How are you feeling? Elspeth had some terrible morning sickness when she was expecting Jonathon."

"I'm feeling very well but a bit bored. If it were up to James, I'd be resting every minute of every day, but as soon as he goes to the Thompson Gymnasium, I have Mr. Bauer take me to my offices at Vermeal Industries. I can never learn everything there is to learn if I don't start immediately. Especially as Mr. Critchfeld, my father's secretary, is set to retire in three months."

"What does James have to say about your trips to Vermeal Industries?"

"What my husband does not know will not hurt him," she said with a hint of a grin.

"True," Muireall replied. "How is Mr. Vermeal taking his secretary's retirement?"

"Not well, as you may imagine. He is like the proverbial bear with a thorn in his paw. I don't know who his 'Androcles' will be, but I will be happy when there is someone in place. So will poor Mr. Critchfeld, who is taking the brunt of his bad humor."

Muireall laughed and poured her sister-in-law more tea. "What brings you out today, especially in this chilly weather?"

"An invitation. I'm hosting a dinner party and wanted to make sure you, Aunt Murdoch, and Payden will attend. I'm hoping Aunt Murdoch will agree to stay with us for a few weeks too. James misses her, and I think she may enjoy a change of scenery.

"And please do bring Captain Marcus and that darling daughter of his. I was telling my aunt's stepchildren—you remember Geoffrey and Susannah, I'm sure—all about her, and Susannah especially would like to meet her. She's decided the two of them could have their dinner with the adults and then escape to play a game or read."

Muireall stared at Lucinda and then dropped her eyes to the pastry in her hand. "I can't imagine why you would invite them. They dined here by chance only. It wasn't as though there was an intentional meeting."

"Of course not. But still, James and I were glad to make the captain's acquaintance. We're not so closed off that we cannot make new friends."

"He is no longer a captain, Lucinda. Just plain old Mr. Marcus." She stared out the front window, in front of which sat the quilting ring and surrounding chairs. She did not want to get to know him any better. She did not want to feel an affinity for him, certainly no more than the respect she felt now. She did not want to feel any more connection than she already did.

"Muireall," Lucinda said in her no-nonsense voice. "What is the matter?"

"Nothing. Nothing at all," she said and turned back to her. "Now tell me all about the nursery. What colors did you finally choose?"

Lucinda was quiet for a moment and then indulged Muireall's change of subject. Shortly, Muireall walked outside with Lucinda, worried she may slip on ice or the slushy snow left over from the recent storm. Mr. Bauer hurried to his mistress's side.

"Let me help you, Mrs. Thompson. If anything was to happen to you, Mr. Thompson would have my hide, he would. I've got warm bricks for your feet and that fur wrap for your lap."

Muireall kissed Lucinda's cheek. "He'll make sure you are home safely and wrapped in a blanket."

Lucinda smiled ruefully and turned to her coachman. "Thank you, Mr. Bauer. You take prodigiously good care of me."

Muireall waved as the carriage pulled away, staring down the street but seeing little. She and Mr. Marcus were being manipulated; however, how could she *not* invite them, knowing that Ann Marcus would be so excited? The last time Muireall had been at the orphanage, she'd spied Mr. Marcus across the street hauling a wagon full of goods to the grocer in the next block. He had been limping heavily, and she'd noticed his ears were bright red with cold. She'd hurried inside the orphanage, lest he noticed her. She did not believe he would like her to see him doing manual labor. Not that he was too proud to do anything to care for his daughter, just that he would most likely prefer not to have her, or anyone, observe him.

LATER THAT WEEK, MR. BAUER PICKED MUIREALL UP AT EIGHT in the morning. She was carrying scarves and mittens for the sisters to give out to the orphans and had a special set of mittens in her coat pocket to match Ann Marcus's scarf. They had been painstakingly lined with flannel by Aunt Murdoch for "that precious girl."

She spent her morning helping some very young children with their letters and was pleased with their progress and how they'd kept her mind occupied instead of dwelling on her coming conversation with Mr. Marcus. She had no idea why she was dreading it. She would merely offer the invitation, and he could choose to accept or decline. That was all there was to it. She stood up from leaning over a small child's shoulder and stretched her back when she heard Ann's lilting voice.

"Miss Thompson! There you are! I have not seen you for days now," she said cheerfully.

"It is very good to see you too, Ann."

Mr. Marcus walked up behind his daughter. "She's going to stay here for a few hours with the sisters while I tend to a job."

"Of course. Would you like to join the history lesson Father Thomas has just begun?"

"Oh yes. I like to hear him tell the stories," Ann said and turned the hallway corner to the makeshift classrooms, waving at her father as she did.

She stared at Mr. Marcus, who was staring just as intently as she.

"It is good to see you, Miss Thompson. You are looking well."

"Thank you, Mr. Marcus. It is good to see you and Ann both."

He hesitated, squeezing a wool cap in his hands, nodded, and then began to turn. "I'll be back in an hour or so for Ann." Muireall reached out her hand, nearly touching his arm. He glanced down and then turned back. "What is it, Miss Thompson?"

Muireall tried to smile casually, but she feared it looked more like a grimace. "I wanted to speak to you of an invitation for you and Ann."

"An invitation?"

"My brother James's wife, Lucinda, is having a casual meal and was hoping you and Ann would join us." He was looking at her strangely. "You see, Lucinda's mother died when she was an infant, and she was raised by her father's sister, her Aunt Louisa. Louisa recently married a man who has several children, and Lucinda told them all about Ann, and the youngest girl, Susannah, is looking forward to meeting her."

He shook his head. "You would like to take Ann to meet your sister-in-law's cousins?"

"Well, you're certainly invited too. We'll have something to eat, and the young people can play some games or sing at the piano. It is this Saturday, the seventeenth."

"I'm not much into social outings, Miss Thompson, but do thank your sister-in-law. It was very gracious of her to remember Ann and me."

"I wish you would reconsider. Ann would enjoy herself, and I think you would as well. Unrelieved burdens can weigh us down. Please come, bring Ann, enjoy a meal, and allow your daughter to meet some new friends."

"Where will I meet new friends, Miss Thompson?" Ann said as she hurried around the corner of the hallway, smiling up at Muireall. "At Locust Street?"

"No. My brother and his wife are having some relatives and guests over for a meal and Mrs. Thompson thought you and your father would enjoy yourselves. There's a young lady a few years older than you who is interested in meeting you."

"Oh yes!" Ann said and looked at her father. "Please do say we can go."

He glared at Muireall. "That was hardly fair, Miss Thompson."

"It was not fair at all." She was tempted to look away from his glower but did not retreat.

He huffed a breath. "Fine," he said and caught Ann as she launched herself at him. "Please tell Mr. and Mrs. Thompson we would be happy to join them."

. . .

Anthony brushed his best jacket and asked Mrs. Phillips to press his one good shirt, although she refused to take his coin. He shined his shoes and trimmed his hair in the mirror above the washstand after he shaved and cleaned his teeth. He remembered how to look and act in rarified company, he thought to himself, and let out a harrumph. Ann had gone downstairs to Mrs. Phillips's apartment to bathe in her tub and have her long hair washed.

He could hear her voice as she came up the steps, singing a nursery rhyme she'd learned at the orphanage. She hurried through the door in her chemise and drawers, wrapped in a blanket, and rushed to the coal stove.

"Mmm, that is nice and warm." She smiled. "I am so looking forward to tonight! Aren't you, Papa? It was so nice of Mr. Thompson's wife to think of us."

"It was," he said as he arranged his four-in-hand tie. He would not comment about Miss Thompson's duplicity in tempting Ann with her description of the evening. Muireall Thompson had put him in an uncomfortable situation, she knew she'd done it, and he had no intentions of staying quiet about the subject, although he doubted he could bring it up that evening. He would not be so gauche as to argue with her while attending a party. But still, the subject was not over.

With his small cash reserve, Anthony had shopped for new stockings for Ann. She was pulling them on now and oohing over how soft and warm they were. He helped her on with her petticoat, although he remembered it was getting short on her and wondered aloud if he should have bought a new one or had her wear the flannel one Miss Thompson had made.

"It is not too short now. Mrs. Phillips made the straps longer, see?" she said and turned her shoulder. "I wish I knew how to sew."

"Very clever. Maybe one of the sisters can teach you to sew. I can sew on a button, but that's about all."

She giggled. "But a button wouldn't have helped my petticoat, would it?"

He couldn't help but smile. She was a joy, a true gift in his life when it would be easy to give up or be grim and hopeless. But he couldn't allow himself the luxury of self-pity. It wouldn't be right in the face of her relentless gladness.

He watched her dry her hair near the stove and then hand him the brush. "If you will just part it straight in the back, I can plait it now all by myself. You'll have to help with the ribbon for my dress, though."

He watched her nimble, slender fingers plaiting her waist-length hair while he knelt in front of her and buckled on her leather boots that he had just polished. He dropped her lavender-colored wool dress over her head and buttoned the back.

"Here." She handed him a long length of purple-and-yellow plaid ribbon. "You will have to make a bow in the back. Or should I take it down to Mrs. Phillips?"

"I can tie my shoelaces, so I should be able to tie this fancy ribbon."

"Oh, Papa! Shoelaces and a satin ribbon are two different things. You mustn't wrinkle the fabric, and do make the loops even."

He smiled and did not ask her where she'd acquired the new ribbon, although he'd seen Muireall Thompson hand her something one afternoon when he was at the orphanage to get her after hauling garbage for the grocer at the corner.

"Even loops? What are you talking about?"

"You're teasing me." She turned when he was done making the bow and wrapped her arms around his neck. "You are the best papa I could ask for. The very best."

He heard the rattle of a carriage near six o'clock and knelt to button Ann's coat. She'd already pulled on her mittens and wrapped the scarf around her neck. She was near giddy with excitement. He held her still at the last moment.

"We must remember our manners tonight, Ann. We will be guests in someone else's home, so the both of us must be on our very best behavior."

She looked at him solemnly. "Yes, Papa. I will do my best."

"I know you will," he said and kissed her forehead. He pulled himself up, holding on to the arm of the sofa.

She held his hand walking down the stairs. Mrs. Phillips opened her door. "Don't you look bright as a new penny!"

"Thank you, Mrs. Phillips."

Anthony smiled at his landlady, who might not be smiling at him next month if he did not have enough to cover his rent. He picked up Ann so she didn't have to wade through the slush to the waiting carriage.

"Mr. Bauer! It is very nice to see you!" Ann said.

"And good to see you, Miss Ann," he said and nodded at Anthony. "I've got hot bricks and blankets in the coach for the ladies."

Anthony put Ann on the seat and then put his foot on the carriage step. It was always difficult to know whether to put his bad foot forward or risk wobbling and maybe falling if his injured leg had to support all of his weight. Mr. Bauer held out his arm and spoke quietly.

"Here you are, sir. Hold my arm."

Anthony glanced at the man, now staring straight ahead. He pushed up, using the man's arm as leverage, and got himself seated on the backward-facing padded bench. The coachman closed the door, called to the man on the back, walked around the carriage to check the door on the other side, and then climbed onto his seat. Ann had a blanket across her lap and was humming a tune. She was beautiful, as beautiful as his wife had been. Yet with no indication of a selfish or corrupted personality, she was exactly the opposite, and in fact reminded him of his sister.

The carriage rocked to a stop at the Thompson house on Locust Street. Young Mr. Thompson was helping the old aunt down the steps. She was making comments that were making him laugh, and behind them Miss Thompson followed.

"Oh, look at Miss Thompson's coat! It is so beautiful!"

Anthony saw it and saw the woman in it too. She was too attractive for her own good in her fitted green coat tucked in at the waist with a dark fur collar and cuffs and large black double-breasted buttons. She had a small green hat on her hair that was piled high on her head, sporting a long pheasant feather, dipping down her back. He got the impression from her clothing, and her brother's black suit with a plaid vest, that this dinner would be more formal than the simple meal and piano singing she'd told him about.

The aunt stepped slowly up the carriage step and sat down beside Ann. "Well, here is my darling girl!"

"And I'm wearing my new scarf and matching mittens!" she said with a laugh.

Miss Thompson climbed in next and sat on the other side of Ann, who was holding hands with the aunt and smiling up at her. Miss Thompson straightened her coat and met his eyes. She did not smile or grin or indicate in any way that she was happy to see him or glad to be going somewhere with him in tow, yet he believed she was. That she was pleased to be with him in a fine carriage on their way to a social event. Together.

The young Thompson climbed in last and plopped down beside him, nodding at him as he did. He looked at Ann.

"Who is the beautiful young lady you've brought with you tonight, Captain? I may steal her away from you."

Ann laughed out loud. "Payden! You must remember me!"

"Ann? Is that you, Ann Marcus?"

Anthony smiled at the young man's teasing and Ann's blushes. It was not long before the carriage turned on a cobbled drive and halted at a large home, windows lit from inside. Two young men hurried to the carriage to help them down. Anthony waited until everyone else had exited and scooted over on the seat, thinking about getting out without falling on his face in the slush.

"Go on, fellows," the coachman said to the two young men. "There's two cases in the boot must be carried inside for Mrs. Murdoch. I'll help this gentleman."

Anthony held on to the offered arm as he stepped down with his good leg, standing still for a few moments to get his bearings and his cane in the right spot to steady him. "Thank you, Mr. Bauer."

The coachman tugged his cap and closed the door.

CHAPTER 4

Muireall bent down and unwound the scarf from Ann's neck. "Give the maid your coat and gloves, dear."

"Thank you," she said and smiled at the young woman.

There were servants everywhere discreetly helping guests with their wraps and directing them to the large room filling with guests, some sitting on sofas and chairs and others standing in groups talking as waiters served drinks. It was a tableau that had troubled her brother James, however recently it seemed he'd given in to his wife, who was wealthy beyond Muireall's understanding. Not that he'd become a snob in any way, but rather just accepting of how his wife managed their home. He was often heard to say, "I have a valet now, damn it to hell."

James had seen them arrive and made his way to them. "Murdoch! My wife has told me you're to stay with us for a week or two. I've already moved a chair and hassock closer to the fire in the small sitting room for you."

"Cheeky brat," she said as she kissed him. "Lucinda insisted, and I thought it might be nice at my age to be waited on from morn until dusk."

James kissed her cheek and directed Payden to where he'd set up a chair for their aunt away from the windows. He shook Mr. Marcus's hand and looked down at Ann, standing at Muireall's side.

"How pretty you look tonight, young lady."

"Oh, thank you, Mr. Thompson. And thank you for inviting me, and my Papa too. Everything is so beautiful," she whispered.

"That is entirely the work of my bride." James smiled. "There are some young cousins of Lucinda's here tonight. Would you like to meet them?"

"Oh yes," she said, looking up at her father. "May I, Papa?"

"Would you like me to come with you?" he asked.

"I'll be fine with Mr. Thompson unless you'd like me to stay with you."

He shook his head, and Ann put her hand in James's. Muireall watched them walk together through the other guests, James stopping to talk to some of them and introducing Ann to everyone, finally picking her up, her arm wrapped around his shoulder, and he laughing at something she said.

"Just a casual meal," Anthony said after a few moments. "I feel as though I've walked into a Chestnut Hill mansion."

"Lucinda's family is quite wealthy. That does not mean she, or my brother James, cannot host a pleasant meal for friends and family."

"No, it does not."

"I get the feeling you are angry with me," she said.

He glanced at her finally. "I promised myself I would not discuss it with you at a party hosted by your family, of which I'm a guest."

A waiter came up to them carrying a tray of wine and champagne. He looked at Mr. Marcus. "If wine is not to your liking, sir, I can get you a whiskey or bourbon."

"Wine will be fine, thank you," he said and turned to her. "Miss Thompson?"

She took a glass of wine from the tray, as did he, and the waiter moved on.

"You look very beautiful tonight, Miss Thompson. Very beautiful."

Muireall didn't breathe for a moment, didn't move, and only after a minute had passed did she meet his eyes. It had been a long time. It had been . . . never. She'd never had a man look at her with admiration the way the Mr. Marcus was doing now.

"Thank you," she finally whispered. She realized then that they'd stepped closer to each other, too close for a public setting such as this but also exactly where she wished to be standing. He glanced away then, as though he realized their nearness too, and took a step back.

"The green suits you better than what you wear to the orphanage."

She smiled. "If this is your attempt at a flirt, then you are rusty, Mr. Marcus."

He glanced at her, stern at first, and then his lips pulled to one side in a half grin. "I suppose you're right."

She looked up and saw Elspeth and Alexander walking toward them. The men shook hands, and they chatted about everyday things. She imagined Elspeth, kind and perceptive Elspeth, sensed that Mr. Marcus may be overwhelmed with the company and the setting. Although she was certain that he'd been reared and educated in a proper home, she thought his natural courtesies may have been stretched to the limit by his recent near poverty. It wasn't long until Lucinda joined them, her father, Henri Vermeal, beside her.

"You are a vision, Miss Thompson," he said and kissed her hand. "It has been far too long since we have seen each other."

"Thank you, Henri. Allow me to introduce Mr. Anthony Marcus to you. Mr. Marcus, Mr. Henri Vermeal is Lucinda's father."

"Mr. Marcus was recently a captain in the Union army, Father," Lucinda said.

"A captain? Who were you with, Marcus?" Henri asked in the brusque manner they were all accustomed to.

"The Forty-Second out of New York."

"You've been out two years or more, then."

Mr. Marcus shook his head. "I stayed on at headquarters. There were still records to maintain and some to make public. Inventories and whatnot."

"And you had a hand in that, Marcus?"

"I did."

Muireall watched the two men, as did Lucinda. There was some underlying masculine current that she was not privy to. Mr. Marcus held himself as if in a military parade, and Henri, although canny with his observations, was assessing him openly.

"Where are Kirsty and Albert, Lucinda?" Muireall asked.

"An important function at the college that Albert had to attend. There is a rumor that he may be named head of his department, and Kirsty felt it wise to support him in all the social settings."

"Kirsty says she has made several friends among the faculty wives and some of the female professors from the Philadelphia Female College."

"Kirsty hobnobbing with professors," Elspeth said. "It defies logic. She is much more suited to talk business with Henri."

The women laughed and turned when Henri spoke.

"Come along, then, Marcus. You too, Pendergast. We will withdraw to the library, where my son-in-law keeps—I mean hides—the good whiskey." He turned and walked toward the door of the room, clearly certain that whomever he'd designated would follow without question.

"Enjoy." Lucinda smiled.

Mr. Marcus glanced at her with a raised brow. Muireall took

the wineglass from his hand as he walked away. "What is that about?"

"I have no idea," Elspeth said. "Do you, Lucinda?"

"Father is always interested in the stories military men will share. He much admires them, although he would never say that outright."

"HAVE A SEAT WHILE I ATTEMPT TO FIND THE SCOTCH WHISKEY that your sister-in-law who sells the fabrics has her Scottish contacts wrap in wool and ship here. Better than what is produced at my own distilleries. It is excellent," Mr. Vermeal said when they entered a small room, its walls lined with books. "Critchfeld is my long-suffering employee, Marcus." He gestured to an older man on one end of the sofa facing the fireplace, who looked to be near a doze. He was plump and soft looking, in direct contrast to Vermeal, who was rail thin and clearly accustomed to being in charge.

"Long-suffering hardly begins to describe my tenure," the man said in a soft voice as he shook Anthony's hand.

"What did you say?" Vermeal asked as he opened cabinets built into the wall below shelves of books.

"The scotch is in the liquor cart, sir," Critchfeld said.

"The liquor cart?"

Critchfeld stood and went to the wooden cart behind the sofa that held a metal ice bin, tongs, and a variety of glassware. He opened the doors and put a bottle beside the glasses and resumed his seat.

"Ah, there it is," Vermeal said as walked to the cart.

Anthony studied the employee, who picked up a cut-crystal glass from the table beside him and took a slow sip. Anthony and Alexander Pendergast each accepted a glass of scotch from Vermeal, who was walking to a chair angled near the fire. He looked at Anthony.

"What prompted you to join the military, Marcus?" Vermeal asked as he seated himself.

Anthony was not certain he liked Mr. Vermeal, but he'd had some commanding officers over the years cut from the same cloth, so he was familiar with the type. In the army, the worst mistake to make with colonels or majors was to capitulate to their wild schemes and be afraid to point out flaws in their reasoning. Officers responsible for thousands of lives did not need men who were unable to challenge them in a respectful way.

"My father was in the military. Served in the Indian Wars. My uncle as well. I grew up believing that was the course I would take as an adult."

"So no altruistic feelings for the Union over the Confederacy," Vermeal replied. "No emotions overriding good sense."

"I wouldn't say that," Anthony said. "I'm not so selfless as to refer to myself as altruistic, however the idea that one person can *own* another person is morally repugnant and worth fighting against."

Vermeal was staring at him, and he had no intention of looking away.

"Slavery goes back to the Bible, Marcus. Surely you are not so arrogant as to believe yourself above Holy Scripture?"

"The Bible, for the most part, was written by men. Men living in extraordinary times, but still men all the same. Slavery is wrong. It always will be."

Vermeal raised his brows. "Firm in your conviction, are you?"

"Yes."

The door of the room opened, and Elspeth Thompson peaked in. "Oh, there you are, Alexander. Lucinda is getting ready to ring the bell for dinner."

The men stood and filed out, Elspeth on the arm of her husband. Anthony walked the long hallway to the dining room beside Vermeal.

"Where are you gainfully employed now?" Vermeal asked.

"I'm not currently employed, although I have been offered a position beginning next month at Endernoff Industries."

Vermeal glanced at him. "Endernoff? He's a fool."

"That may prove true, however it is employment for a man with little industry experience and a marked limp. I am grateful for the opportunity."

"I doubt your gratitude will last," Vermeal replied.

MUIREALL WAITED NEAR HER SEAT IN THE DINING ROOM, watching for Mr. Marcus to appear. She did not want him to feel he'd been abandoned, and she was terribly curious as to why he'd been gone so long with Henri and Alexander. She saw him come in and veer toward her as Henri stopped Lucinda.

"Where is Ann?"

"She is seated at the smaller table near the windows with the other young people. We've been seated here, Mr. Marcus," she said. Just as he began to pull out her chair, Lucinda came by with two place cards in hand.

"Muireall? Mr. Marcus? Would you mind terribly moving to the other table? I just found out that the Bentons are not on good terms with the Andersons and would like to move them to these two seats. Do you mind?"

Muireall shook her head. "Whatever makes your hostessing easier is fine with me. Mr. Marcus?"

"I haven't a clue who either party are, so it makes no difference to me. Lead the way."

They followed Lucinda to the other long table set for twenty guests to two empty chairs beside Mr. Vermeal, who was seated at the head of that table. She kissed Muireall's cheek and thanked her.

Mr. Marcus leaned down to her once she was seated. "I'm going to check on Ann."

She nodded and looked at Henri.

"Devoted to his daughter?" he asked.

"Yes. Very much so."

"Where did you meet him, Muireall?"

She glanced at him, wondering of his interest. "His daughter sometimes stays at the orphanage where I volunteer. You remember, don't you, Henri? You've given generously to the Sisters of Charity."

"Oh yes. Lucinda was telling me you brought home the daughter to Locust Street when he was late returning to the orphanage and bought his wrath."

"Hardly wrath," she said. "But he was worried and a bit panicked."

Mr. Marcus pulled out his chair and seated himself. "Your youngest brother apparently volunteered to sit with the young people, although he was to have a seat with the adults. Ann is seated beside him and in raptures. She dismissed me with a kiss and a wave. I fear I've been usurped."

"It happens before you know it, Marcus. You turn around and your perfect and beautiful daughter is marrying a boxer with a crooked nose."

Muireall laughed. "You must admit, Henri, Lucinda and James are a love match."

Henri shrugged and concentrated on his wineglass, which had just been filled. "I admit nothing. However, he is devoted to my daughter and he will be to this grandchild of mine as well."

"What does Vermeal Industries produce, Mr. Vermeal?" Mr. Marcus asked as the cream-of-leek soup was served.

Henri studied Mr. Marcus for a moment.

"Little here in the United States. Most industries owned outright are in France, Britain, and Spain. Wine and glassware in France, spices primarily in Spain, and Scotch whiskey and locomotive parts on the island. Our investments here are in new inventions and commodities providing capital to upstart industries."

Mr. Marcus held a spoon full of soup halfway to his mouth, listening intently to Henri's recitation.

"Quite an assortment. Is there a common thread?"

Henri smiled. "Yes. They all make me money."

Mr. Marcus chuckled and then quickly stood, as did Henri, when an impressively buxom and very beautiful brunette walked to the chair on Henri's left. "My dear Henri! I am so fortunate to be seated beside you!"

"Mrs. Dorchester, you are looking very fine this evening, madam," Henri said, oozing charm as he kissed her hand. "Allow me to introduce you to Miss Thompson and Mr. Marcus."

Lucinda had told her that there were many women, young and old, vying to be the next Mrs. Vermeal, although her father been a widow since Lucinda's birth. But he'd always had a hostess in his sister, Louise, until she'd recently married her childhood sweetheart and was no longer able to direct staff and plan the more intricate parts of his entertaining. Lucinda filled in when she could, but she was busy with her own home and husband. Muireall had often thought Henri may be lonely, rattling around the Vermeal mansion with just servants as company.

"Miss Thompson? You are related to Henri's dear daughter, Lucinda, I believe."

"I am. She married my brother James."

"Oh yes. I was introduced to Mr. Thompson in the receiving line. Quite a . . . large fellow, isn't he?"

Muireall smiled at the woman's comment. "He's a boxer. A champion too, although retired from the ring. He's part owner and manager of the Thompson Gymnasium and Athletic Studio."

"I have never in all of my days seen a man's hands move as fast as his did during his last match," Henri said and looked at Muireall. "He is formidable in the ring."

"James would be grateful for your comment," she said.

"I doubt that," he replied and turned his attention to Mrs.

Dorchester as she leaned his direction, displaying her vast womanly charms.

She glanced at Mr. Marcus, who was busy cutting the beef course or trying not to notice the woman across the table whose breasts were now lying on Henri's outstretched arm.

"The dinner is excellent," he said. "I doubt if Ann will be able to eat everything and is probably wrapping what she can't finish in one of these linen napkins."

Muireall chuckled. "She is always looking for your next meal."

"I will get things righted when I begin this job."

"Of course you will."

"Ann is outgrowing her dresses, and once I have received a pay, I was hoping you would take her to get one or two new ones."

"I would love to. One or two ready-made dresses and then Aunt Murdoch and I can make simple dresses for every day for her." She looked at him. "You can purchase the fabric from my sister Kirsty for a very good price."

"I'm not talking about charity."

"I never mentioned charity."

Mr. Marcus could be prickly but also charming and always well-mannered. She would ask him someday about his upbringing. Maybe. If she ever had an opportunity to be alone with him again. She admitted to herself she'd enjoyed his escort immensely. He stood when Henri did and helped her from her seat.

"I could have eaten some of Mrs. McClintok's bread pudding," he whispered close to her ear.

"Don't worry. Lucinda told me she is serving dessert from a buffet and coffee and spirits with it."

"Papa?" Ann said from his side.

"Yes, Ann. Are you enjoying yourself?"

"Oh yes! This is Susannah, Mrs. Thompson's cousin. We are going to go to the music room. Susannah plays the piano!"

"And skip dessert? I can hardly believe it of you, Ann Marcus," he said with his hand over his heart.

Ann giggled. "We will not be skipping dessert. Mrs. Thompson has asked the cook to make us a tray of desserts and lemonade."

"Then you'd best get to it," he said and then sobered. "And mind your manners, dear."

"Oh yes, Papa! I will."

Muireall watched her hurry away, hand in hand with Susannah Delgado. "She is a precious child."

"She is," he replied. "She's my anchor. The reason I get myself out of bed and do my best to stay cheerful."

"Let us find our way to the sweets, sir."

Mr. Marcus winged his arm, and she wrapped her hand around it. How many years had it been since she'd been escorted anywhere by someone other than her brothers? Muireall glanced at him as they walked the hallway with the rest of the guests.

Anthony Marcus was gentlemanly. He was honorable and bright and masculine to his core. And she was in danger of losing her heart to him, even with their short acquaintance, she admitted to herself. Though more disturbing than feeling unreturned regard was her attraction to him. She had no experience with sexual congress or even kissing. Was she contemplating that? Sexual congress? She blushed even thinking about what would be involved.

Henri waylaid Mr. Marcus as soon as they entered the room. "There are some men I'd like to introduce you to. Come with me."

"In a moment, Mr. Vermeal," he said and turned to her. "Would you like me to get you some dessert or tea?"

She smiled at Henri's impatience, although she could not understand why he was insistent on monopolizing Mr. Marcus's time. "Elspeth is there with some other women at the dessert table. Join the men, why don't you, and I'll join the ladies."

He executed a half bow. "I'll be with you shortly because I have no intention of missing any of the desserts."

She walked across the room to her sister and glanced back. He had waited near the door until she joined Elspeth and then turned to Henri with a nod, following him to a group of older men, all business types, from what she could tell. How gentlemanly he was to wait until she'd arrived at her destination of several women. How unique for someone to be so concerned for her comfort! It was what she thought marriage should be like, and that sentiment had been proven true in how her married siblings conducted themselves with their spouses.

"How is Mr. Marcus enjoying himself?" Elspeth asked.

"I believe he has had some experience with finer entertainments and manners. I do wonder why Lucinda's father has been so attentive to him. It's not like Henri is chummy with anyone."

"So true. Maybe he is just trying to set Mr. Marcus at ease." Muireall glanced at Elspeth, who laughed. "No, I suppose not."

Lucinda and her Aunt Louisa joined them, bringing a woman and a younger woman with her. "Please meet friends of ours, Mrs. Roberta Binginham and her daughter, Alice."

After pleasantries and introductions had been made, Muireall asked Lucinda's Aunt Louisa, now Louisa Delgado, how married life was for her.

Louisa sparkled. "It is everything I wanted and dreamed of, Muireall. Renaldo is attentive and kind, and I adore his children. We have a lovely home, and Geoffrey and Susannah have adapted well to their new country, especially as their oldest sister, Millicent, is not too far from them."

"I am so very happy for you," Muireall said, feeling just the slightest pang of jealousy. The others were talking among themselves, and Muireall turned a bit, shielding what she wanted to ask from other's views. "What a change, though, for you. I mean, well, you and I have been unmarried all our adult life. It must have been an adjustment."

Louisa leaned close and whispered, "If you are asking about the intimate aspects, then I must tell you it has been a revelation.

It is a joyous facet of love that has only made our relationship stronger."

Muireall stared at her and then away, realizing what she'd missed, what she would always miss. She felt tears gather. "I'm very happy for you."

"Oh dear," Louisa said. "I did not mean to make you sad. Let us speak of something else. The young lady that is spending the evening with Susannah is darling and so polite. Tell me again how she is related to your family?"

"Ann is not related to the Thompsons," Muireall said and related the story of Ann dining with them and her father's arrival and introduction as Captain Marcus.

"Oh," Louisa said and looked speculatively at Muireall. "Her father appears to be a very commanding gentleman. Handsome too."

"I hadn't noticed."

Louisa trilled a laugh. "You are a poor liar, Muireall Thompson. And here he comes, looking thunderous."

"Mr. Marcus? Have you had any desserts?" Muireall asked.

"They do not allow desserts when you are subject to an inquisition."

Louisa laughed. "My brother set his sights on you this evening, I think?"

"Allow me to introduce you. Mr. Marcus, Mrs. Louisa Delgado, Lucinda's aunt and Mr. Vermeal's sister."

"I am sorry if he waylaid you, but Henri does like to hear soldier's perspectives on the War Between the States," Louisa said.

"Strange, then, that I was introduced and promptly ignored."

"No one spoke to you?"

"Other than the courtesies, no. They talked of the Franco Prussian War and labor problems here in the States."

"Probably an interesting conversation, though," Louisa said. "I recognize some of those men. Hamilton Fish's Under-Secretary of

State, Mr. Davis, is the white-haired one, and the man to his right is Joseph Potts, who is a major stockholder in the Pennsylvania Railroad."

"That's rich company to be sure for just a family dinner," he said and glanced at Muireall.

"It is rather a small affair. Some of Henri's cohorts finagle any opportunity to meet James Thompson. It galls Henri to no end!" Louisa laughed. "With all their money, you would think they wouldn't be worshipful of personages in the sporting world, but they are. Oh, they are!"

CHAPTER 5

Anthony sat across from Muireall Thompson in the carriage on the way to Devlin Street, holding a sleeping Ann on her lap. He'd tried to lift his daughter from her, and she'd eyed him in a way that made him sit back in his seat. The coach pulled up to the Locust Street home, and the young brother climbed out.

"Tell Mrs. McClintok I'll be back shortly after we've seen the Mr. Marcus home," she said through the open door.

Anthony moved over to sit beside her. "Here. I'll take her. You needn't make the trip."

She glared at him. "This child is exhausted. I won't disturb her."

"She will be asleep in two shakes after I take her in my arms."

Mr. Bauer stood outside the carriage, waiting to help her down.

"Close the door, Mr. Bauer. Please take us to Mr. Marcus's lodgings."

"Yes, ma'am," he said and climbed back on the coach.

The streets were dark as they neared his neighborhood other than the occasional flash of moonlight, so it took him some time to notice she was struggling to fix Ann's hat. He leaned around her, picking the hat up from where it hung on her other side. He glanced at her, realizing he was quite close to her. Close enough to hear her shallow breathing and smell the soap she used for her hair. Close enough to see her pink cheeks and feel her chest rise and fall in time with his. He studied her eyes when the light was bright enough and glanced at her lips, parted now, as if waiting for his. He was tempted, sorely tempted, to kiss her. He was not sure of how the attraction between them had flickered, but there was no doubt it was a flame now.

Her lips were just inches from his, and he wished that so many things in his life were different. That his body was whole and that he was respectfully employed. Wishing he was a young, unmarried suitor begging for her hand. But if he'd never married, he wouldn't have his precious daughter. He leaned closer still, and she closed her eyes.

Ann sighed and settled farther into Miss Thompson's arms. He sat back, calming his body and convincing himself that the very last thing he needed in his life was an entanglement with a woman. The very last thing.

"We're close. Best wake her up as I can't carry her up the steps," he said softly.

Miss Thompson kissed Ann's forehead. "Mr. Bauer can carry her."

"I don't want to wake her either, but she's my responsibility. Ann?" he said softly. "Wake up, dear."

The carriage stopped, and the door opened, Mr. Bauer at the ready.

"Will you carry her inside, Mr. Bauer?" Miss Thompson said.

"Of course, ma'am. Jensen? Get down off your perch and help the gentleman down."

Anthony led the way to his door, key in hand, turning finally to Miss Thompson with a bow. "It was truly a pleasure spending the evening with you and your family. The dinner was delicious, and Ann enjoyed herself very much. Good night."

He opened his door, letting Bauer pass by carrying Ann. Miss Thompson followed. "You needn't come up."

"Certainly, I will need to come up. Who will get her ready for bed?"

"I was going to let her sleep in her dress."

She stared at him until he stepped back from the doorway. He hated, absolutely hated, her seeing his cramped room, with the small stove that heated it and their food beside the faded couch and chair. But he hurried behind her to direct Mr. Bauer to the bed in the alcove closed off with a curtain.

"Here, Mr. Bauer. Lay her down here," he said and moved past him, pulling back the curtains and the heavy blanket. He dug in the jar on the shelf above the dishes for a coin. "Thank you." He held out the tip.

"Thank you for the thought, sir, but I could never accept money from a member of the Thompson family. Wouldn't be right, and Mr. Thompson pays me very well so's I don't have to rely on kindness to put bread on my table."

Anthony dropped his hand to his side. "I'm not a member of the Thompson family."

Bauer glanced at Miss Thompson. "Close enough, sir. I'll be waiting in the carriage, ma'am."

She stepped around the curtain and began to unbuckle Ann's shoes and maneuvered her enough to remove her hat, coat, and dress. "Is there warm water in your kettle?"

"Yes," he said as he touched the side of it. He watched her bustle around, finding a rag on the shelf with his shaving kit, filling the wash basin with water and soaping up the rag.

She wiped Ann's face, her eyes fluttering open, as she did.

"Oh, Miss Thompson," Ann whispered. "That feels ever so good."

"Let me wipe your hands," Miss Thompson said softly. "There's some leftover cake between your fingers, I think."

Ann smiled as her eyes closed. Miss Thompson pulled the

blankets up and tucked them tightly around her. What a marvelous mother she would be.

"Where do you sleep, Mr. Marcus?" she asked as she looked around the room.

"That seems like a very personal question, Miss Thompson."

"I'm so sorry. I didn't mean to . . ."

I was teasing you," he said and smiled. I usually sleep on the sofa unless it is bitter cold, then I sleep with Ann. But she is getting too old for that, isn't she?"

"Sometimes needs must."

"I thank you for the invitation and for convincing me to go this evening. I did enjoy myself and got to indulge in excellent spirits and good food, and even though Mr. Vermeal dominated some of my time, it was enjoyable to be hearing about world affairs and business matters. I can't discuss that sort of thing with Ann, of course. And she enjoyed herself immensely, and it seemed she conducted herself well."

"She did very well, and I had several people compliment her in my hearing."

"Good. That is good to hear."

"I should be going," she said, though she hesitated. She walked directly to him then, kissed his cheek, and hurried out the door.

He did not move, not even to lock the door. He was still contemplating what a wonderful end to the evening her gesture was, and he imagined that it had taken considerable courage on her part. She was not effusive, her affection would never shout but would be as heartfelt as someone who stood on a mountaintop to declare their feelings, perhaps even more. He'd already entertained inappropriate thoughts about her, and he was certain those inclinations were not one-sided.

MUIREALL SAT BESIDE ANN AT THE SISTERS OF CHARITY Orphanage, reviewing the paper that she'd asked Ann to write about Roman emperors. Ann had done well considering the few books available at the orphanage. Muireall would like to take her to the library sometime, if her father would allow it. She thought Ann would love it. She looked up when the front door of the orphanage opened and Mr. Marcus's landlady, Mrs. Phillips, came inside and walked directly to them. Muireall stood in anticipation of some news, probably not good news.

"There you are, Ann, dear. Come along home. Hurry and get your coat," Mrs. Phillips said.

"What has happened?" Muireall asked.

"Mr. Marcus fell and hurt his leg. His good leg. Hurry now, Ann."

As Muireall helped Ann with her coat, she was silent but tense, meeting Muireall's eyes with worry. Muireall donned her own coat and told the sisters she'd be leaving for the day.

"Come along, Ann," she said. "Let us see how your father fares."

"Papa," Ann whispered, and tears filled her eyes.

"Don't borrow trouble," Muireall said with less surety and more hopefulness. "I'm sure he's fine."

When they reached the boarding house, Muireall followed Ann upstairs and stopped Mrs. Phillips at the door. "I will report to you as soon as I've gotten Ann settled. I can't thank you enough for getting us from the orphanage."

The landlady wrung her hands. "I do so adore that child, and Mr. Marcus is such a gentleman. So kind, always offering to help me with small fixes and to deal with the laborers if I've got a bigger repair. He's a godsend after my Jimmy up and decided to go west. Tell me if there's anything to be done."

"I will, Mrs. Phillips. I just think the less people to see him when he's not at his best would suit him better."

"You're right, Miss Thompson. He's a man with a man's pride."

Muireall went into the Marcus apartment. He was stretched out flat on his back on the couch, a trickle of blood above his ear.

"Oh, Papa! You're bleeding," Ann said. "Let me help you."

"You can help me by being quiet. My head is pounding. Do not fret now. Your Papa will be fine; he'll just need a day or two to rest." He looked up at Muireall. "Why are you here?"

Muireall turned to Ann. "Ann, will you please go downstairs with Mrs. Phillips? She is worried sick about your father. You can reassure her that he will be fine. Also, take this coin and send one of the orphans—Tommy, perhaps—for a bag of coal. Ask Mrs. Phillips to watch you cross the street to the orphanage."

"I don't need . . ." Mr. Marcus began sharply but then reached down to his leg, clearly in severe pain.

"Go on, Ann. I'll keep your father company." Ann hurried out the door, coin in hand, wiping her eyes on her sleeve.

"I have no need of your company, Miss Thompson. I would prefer you leave."

Muireall knelt on the floor near his head. "I'm going to help you sit up so I can get your jacket off of you." She slipped her hand under his shoulders and lifted, hearing his intake of breath on the pain. She shrugged his coat down his arms and helped him lay back. She moved down to his feet and began to unlace his boots.

"You absolutely will not remove my boots! Do you hear me?"

"The sisters half a block away can hear you. Quit fidgeting."

A knock sounded at the door, and Muireall said come in as Mr. Marcus shouted to go away. The door creaked open, and Mr. Bauer stuck his head in.

"Miss Thompson? Is there anything I can do for you? The sisters told me you were here."

"No!" Mr. Marcus shouted.

"Yes, Mr. Bauer. How fortuitous your timing is. Please go to the University of Penn to Cohen Hall. Dr. Albert Watson is a researcher there. Please ask him to attend me here."

"Yes, ma'am," Mr. Bauer said over the shouting.

Mr. Marcus stopped yelling suddenly, and Muireall saw his face go white. "I'm going to be sick."

Muireall retrieved a basin and was barely back to his side when he retched. She wrung out a wet towel and wiped his face and hands, now shaking with his efforts. She poured him a glass of water and told him to rinse his mouth.

"Where is the water closet, Mr. Marcus?"

"In the hallway," he whispered through pale lips.

Muireall carried the basin to the water closet in the hallway and returned to see him breathing deeply as if to stave off pain.

She wrestled his left boot from his foot and saw an ugly gash peeking up over his sock and bruising already beginning. She untied his right boot to his feeble protests and carefully removed it. There were dark scars crisscrossing his foot and ankle and an area above his ankle that seemed to be missing flesh and muscle. She could even see the shape of his leg bone. It was a terrible-looking wound.

"Seen enough?" he said.

"Unbutton your pants and lift your hips, Mr. Marcus."

"I will not, you infernal, interfering woman!"

"Unbutton your pants, or I will do it for you. I'm sure you have short drawers on underneath, and these pants are soaking wet and muddy."

"You are the most infuriating woman I've ever met," he said as he began to unbutton his pants.

"Do you have a pair of long drawers or more comfortable pants anywhere here?"

"On the shelf behind me," he said.

Muireall allowed him his privacy, even though it cost him dearly to get his pants off by himself. She found a pair of drawstring pants and helped him on with them. He was out of breath and white-faced by the time she had him situated on a pillow, in clean pants, and under a blanket.

"Do not go to sleep, Mr. Marcus. I don't know if you have a concussion or not."

"What do you know of nursing?" he said irritably.

"My brother James, the boxer. I've patched him up more times than you know."

She puttered around the room, straightening blankets and anything she could do to keep her hands occupied until she heard voices on the steps and opened the door. "Albert. I'm so sorry to pull you away from your work. In here please."

"Thank the d-dear Lord you are well, Muireall. I wasn't sure."

"I am well, Albert. Mr. Marcus, whom you've met as an . . ."

"I slipped on ice, Dr. Watson. There was no need for Miss Thompson to bother you. I'll be fine in a thrice."

"If you wouldn't mind, Muireall, please step out into the hallway. I'd like to examine Mr. Marcus."

Muireall stared at Albert, but he turned away from her and began talking softly to Mr. Marcus. She went out to the landing on the top of the steps, where Ann was waiting.

"He is a doctor?" she asked.

"Yes. He is married to my younger sister Kirsty. Do you remember him from when you had dinner with us?"

She nodded. "Papa doesn't engage doctors often. They are very expensive, he says."

"You mustn't worry about a fee. It will all work out. It is more important that your father is well."

"Yes, of course. I'll say a prayer."

Muireall watched her squeeze her eyes shut, her lips moving with her words. She hugged her close and kissed the top of her head. Tommy was back with coal just as the door opened. Ann took Tommy inside to show him where to put the coal. Muireall looked up at Albert.

"Well?"

"I don't think he is c-concussed, although he did bang his head very hard on the pavement. He should be woken once an hour tonight. I stitched the gash in his leg, only needed a few, and cleaned all the other contusions. I also think he would benefit from some exercises for his damaged leg. Someone should stay here with him t-tonight. Another adult. Not just the daughter."

Muireall glanced down the steps. "Mr. Bauer? Would you consider staying with Mr. Marcus tonight? He will need to be woken every hour. I can speak to my brother if you are concerned about what he would say."

"Mr. Thompson will not care. Jensen will be available if necessary, although they rarely travel in the evening during the week. I'll have to stop home and tell my son, ma'am."

"Very good, and thank you," she said as he turned to the door. "Mr. Marcus will not care for my plans, I suspect."

Albert smiled. "He did imply you could be rather b-bossy."

"Did he now? And what did you say?"

"I told him the Thompson women all were and he'd b-best get used to it!" Albert laughed.

She raised her brows, but Albert just shifted his black leather bag from one hand to the other so he could kiss her cheek.

"Thank you, Albert."

He waved as he hurried down the steps. Muireall took a breath and opened the door to Mr. Marcus's rooms. "Ann? Please check with Mrs. Phillips for me. She said she'd be making some soup for you."

Ann ran out the door, eager to help, and Muireall turned to the patient, who was glaring at her. "How are you feeling?"

"My head hurts like the devil, and the ointment Dr. Watson used on the stitches he did on my leg stings as if on fire. I am weak and stiff and do not care for your interference."

"You would rather have had a terrified eight-year-old trying to help you? What if infection settled on your good leg or you fell into a coma from a concussion?"

"Dr. Watson said I am not concussed."

"Don't, Mr. Marcus. Don't wrap yourself in your pride and embarrassment to the detriment of yourself and Ann."

The wind seemed to leave his sails then as he took a deep breath and closed his eyes. "I don't care for being incapacitated."

"No one does, and you most certainly will not like what I'm going to tell you next."

"Are you going to parade me down Devlin Street in my short drawers? Because at this point, anything else will be bearable."

"Good. Then I've arranged, per my brother-in-law's orders, that someone stay with you tonight. Mr. Bauer has agreed to and knows he must wake your prickly self every hour to make sure you've not gone off from us."

He opened one eye. "And?"

"And Ann will be staying with me on Locust Street."

"I suppose that is for the best, although it all galls me to no end. It was just a little slip and fall and the ignominy of being hauled home by two strangers. If the grocer had not loaded my arms so full, I would have seen the ice on the walkway."

"Accidents do happen."

"Come here, Miss Thompson. Please?"

She went to the sofa and knelt near him. He picked up her hand from where it lay by his side and kissed her knuckles. "I thank you for everything you've done for me. Truly, I wouldn't know what to do, and Ann would worry. I'm sorry to be such a poor patient."

He stared into her eyes, and she could not stop tears from forming.

"My dear Muireall. You were worried too. If I were whole . . ."

She stood quickly when she heard Ann's and Mrs. Phillips's voices in the hall.

CHAPTER 6

Muireall came down the stairs at the Locust Street house just as a knock sounded at the door. "Mr. Marcus! Come in! You are feeling well enough to be out?"

He smiled at her, the smile she'd seen when he'd teased her, and it made him more attractive than even what her imagination had contrived. Her memories of his bare legs and knees kept her awake many an evening after saying her prayers. She wanted to touch them. But one could hardly say to a gentleman, *I want to touch your naked legs*.

"Miss Thompson." He nodded before stepping across the threshold. "I hope I'm not bothering you."

"Of course not," she said. "Not at all."

He reached into his pocket and pulled out her black gloves. "I've come to return these to you. I believe you left them in our rooms last week after I'd fallen and you'd come to my rescue."

"Thank you. Can I offer you coffee or tea, Mr. Marcus? Please do come sit down."

"Not today. But I thank you for your help and for keeping Ann for those days. She thoroughly enjoyed herself, and it was for the best that I did not try and manage her before my leg was healed."

She tilted her head and smiled. "That is quite an admission, Mr. Marcus."

"Are you determined to make me beg for your favor, then?" he asked and took a step closer to her.

She was unsure why those words aroused certain feelings, but suddenly her collar and corset seemed overly tight. She glanced at him, feeling her face heat in a blush.

"That didn't come out very politely, did it? My apologies. It's just that I've spent some hours over the last week as I lay stretched out on my sofa, reliving that peck on the cheek you bestowed on me the evening of your brother's party."

"Have you?" she whispered.

"I have, Muireall."

He stepped closer, leaned in, and laid his lips softly against her cheek. Her eyes closed, and she let herself bask in his nearness, his masculinity, the smell of soap and the heat of his breath against her cheek. She felt womanly and desired, a new experience for her. She laid her hands on his chest as he moved back, and she stood on her tiptoes to reach her lips to his.

They stood still, barely touching, his breath coming soft against hers. He turned his head and pressed his lips to hers. She felt the intimacy of it all the way to her toes. Her lips parted, he covered her mouth with his, and she found herself against the closed door, arms wrapped around his waist, straining to return his kisses, the full length of his body against hers.

"Muireall," he whispered. "You are so beautiful. So good. I'm not worthy of you."

She kissed him again, feeling bold and worldly. "You are the honorable one. A man determined to do the right thing for his family regardless of the cost."

His hips were pressed firmly against hers, her breasts tight against his chest. She'd never experienced anything quite like it, and she knew this may be her only chance. Her one opportunity with a man she respected and cared for. Why should she wonder her entire life what it was to be enthralled by a man?

"Aunt Murdoch is at James and Lucinda's. Mrs. McClintok is off with Mr. Bamblebit for the day, and Payden is working for Kirsty at her shop."

He stepped back and ran a hand through his hair. "You are alone here, then?"

She nodded. "*We* are alone."

"What are you saying, Muireall?"

She cleared her throat. "I'm saying we could go up those steps. Together."

"No. I won't be so craven as to give in to what may be fleeting desire on your part. I won't."

She stepped away and took his hand in hers, leading him to the staircase. "There is nothing fleeting about my desire. I have never felt anything like this in all my years. I want you, Anthony. Won't you indulge me?"

"Muireall, I desire you as I've never desired a woman before."

"Then fulfill that desire as I will my own."

He stared at her for some long moments and then followed her up the steps and into her room. She waited until he was beside her and locked the door. She kept expecting to panic, to come to her senses, to beg him to release her from a frivolous plan, but it did not happen. Now that he was here beside her, in her room, the one rarely entered by any other than Mrs. McClintok with a dust rag, she felt as if he was in her world, her retreat. A private space where she could be with this man, just the two of them. She hesitated as he leaned back against her closed door.

"I do not know what to do," she said.

"But I do, my darling. I do." He stepped closer and pulled the pins from her hair, letting it fall in heavy waves down her back. "I have dreamt about seeing your hair down. My dreams don't compare."

He unbuttoned his jacket and shrugged it off, along with his four-in-hand tie, leaving a vee of skin at the top of his shirt visible to her. She thought then he might be waiting for her and reached up with shaking fingers to unbutton her shirtwaist. He took hold of both of her hands.

"Muireall. We don't have to do this. There is nothing done that cannot be dismissed. We can—"

She slid out of his grasp and pulled the blankets down to the foot of the bed. "I am nervous because I don't wish to appear gauche and unpracticed, but I am not afraid or having any regrets."

He walked to her and slid his hands into her hair, holding her face still below his. "You're certain?"

"Very."

"Then we will indulge ourselves," he said and stared into her eyes. He touched the buttons of her blouse, a question in his gaze.

She nodded, feeling her breath quicken and her skin heat. He was touching her, grazing her breasts with the backs of his hands as he worked the front of her blouse open. He undid her cuffs and pushed it over her shoulders. He bent down and kissed her ear, her shoulder, and her neck. Soft touches with his lips that made her shiver. She reached for the buttons on her skirt, hidden in her pocket, and let it slide over her hips to the floor.

Anthony pulled his shirt over his head in a rush and sat to pull off his boots. He looked up at her with a half-smile as he stood. "Are you going to unbutton my trousers today as you did on one other memorable occasion?"

But she could not quite process his jest as she couldn't move her eyes from his chest, covered in dark hair and rippling with muscle, his long arms relaxed at his sides. She glanced at his face, untied her petticoats, and stepped out of them. He knelt and unbuckled her shoes, taking his time to roll down her stockings and kiss her inner thigh as he did. When he stood, she did what she wanted to do, undoing her loose everyday corset and pulling her chemise over her head, dropping her drawers to her feet, exposing herself, all of her, to him.

He hitched a breath and growled. "You are every man's dream, Muireall. Your body is perfect."

"I don't want to be *every* man's dream," she whispered.

Their eyes met, and something passed between them, something intimate and telling, without any formal declarations. She was his, she realized at that moment, and it was doubtful she would ever do this with any other man, nor could she imagine it with any other man.

He reached out and touched her breast, and she gasped with pleasure as he held her in his hand. "Lay down, dear. Let us get comfortable."

She stretched out on her bed, waiting for him and watching his every move as he unbuttoned his pants. He sat down on the bed to remove them over his injured foot. He turned and crawled to her, smiling, until he was hovering over her.

"Touch me, Muireall," he whispered. "Touch me wherever you'd like."

She laid her hands on his flanks, and his eyes closed. She glanced down at his manhood, jutting out from dark hair, and reached for him. He dragged in a ragged breath and moaned as she slid her hand over the silky skin. She touched the sac below it, and his hips arched against her.

"It's been a very long time for me, Muireall."

"It's been never for me," she whispered. "Whatever happens will be a most precious memory."

ANTHONY KISSED HER THEN, HARD, OPEN-MOUTHED, AND SHE returned his ardor as he stroked her breast and rubbed her nipple with his thumb. She truly was every man's dream with large, full breasts, a tucked waist, and round hips. He touched her intimately, feeling her wet heat, and spread her legs wide. He must take his time as she was clearly untouched, but he could not stop himself from rubbing his cock against her there. She was moaning and bucking under him already.

He leaned down on one elbow and stroked her face with his free hand. "Are you ready, love?"

She nodded, frenzied, rubbing herself on him. He guided himself to her opening and slid home, feeling resistance and pushing through until he was fully seated. *Dear God!* This was Muireall, his woman, beneath him, moaning and undulating against him. He moved in her slowly but soon unable to control himself, losing the slow pace he'd set for quick thrusts. He did not wait long for her to find her pleasure, watching her as she closed her eyes with a gasp and her legs opened fully. His back arched with his release and he dropped onto her, covering her body completely, his head tucked against her auburn hair spread on the pillow behind her.

He stayed in place for a minute, breathing hard, and then, realizing his whole weight was on her, rolled to his back, bringing her with him. She sighed.

They both must have fallen asleep for a short while because when his eyes opened, she was laid tight against his side, breathing softly, her head on his chest. He kissed her forehead.

"Muireall, love. Wake up," he whispered.

She lifted her head, looked at him, and smiled shyly. "Anthony."

"I don't think we slept long, but it would probably be best if we got ourselves up and dressed before any of your family comes home."

"I would like to stay here in bed with you all day and forget the rest of the baking. You must take a loaf with you when you go."

"There's nothing I would like more," he said and kissed her slow, with languid passion.

They stood reluctantly. She was suddenly shy, this beautiful, sensuous woman, picking up her clothes and hurrying behind a dressing screen. He chuckled.

"Don't laugh at me, Anthony," she said. "I've no experience with this!"

He was pulling on his jacket when she stepped out from behind the screen, looking again like a proper lady, her hair neat and her clothes just so. He took up his cane, which he'd dropped the moment he came into her room, and walked to her. He bowed and held out his hand. She placed hers in his, and he kissed the back of it.

"I was not prepared for this interlude. It is possible there could be consequences, Muireall. You must tell me immediately if there is," he said.

For the briefest moment, her eyes lit with hope and longing but disappeared quickly. "I don't imagine that one time will result in anything momentous."

"Of course it is momentous, darling. We've been intimate. You've given yourself to me and I to you," he said suddenly feeling the weight of their actions, although he was not fearful or regretful. But joyous. He'd found the woman who was precious above all others. "We have much to discuss."

"It was not my intent to trap you, Anthony. Never." She looked away and walked to the door. "Come, and I will wrap a loaf of freshly baked bread for you."

"A union with you will never be a trap," he said as they went down the hallway.

He followed her, taking his time on the steps and she waiting politely. He stepped down beside her on the first landing and wrapped his free arm around that perfect waist of hers, pulling her tight against him. She came willingly and looked at him, dreamy eyed and vulnerable. He prayed she would always look at him that way. He kissed her then, sliding his tongue in her mouth as her arms came around his neck.

"We must stop or we'll be—" he whispered.

The front door of the house opened.

"Oh. Oh dear. I will come back another time," Lucinda Thompson said.

MUIREALL HURRIED DOWN THE LAST STEPS TO THE FOYER, HER cheeks flaming. She could not think of what to say; she could not think at all! "Oh. Oh. Lucinda!"

Lucinda smiled and clasped Muireall's hands. "How good it is to see you. We've had no time to talk about my party. Could we have some tea? Won't you join us, Mr. Marcus?"

"Perhaps . . ."

"Please do. The reason I came by is twofold. I was to give Muireall a message for her to pass on to you," she said and started down the hallway. "Is the kettle warm?"

"I . . . I don't know," Muireall said and hurried after her.

"Then I will see to our tea while you show Mr. Marcus to a seat," she said, smiling as if she had not just seen them engaged in a passionate embrace halfway to the second floor. There was really no conclusion other than him having been in her bedroom.

Muireall went into parlor, Anthony behind her. She plopped down onto the sofa, and he continued to the quilting ring near the window. "Oh dear. This is terrible. What was I thinking?" she said.

"Terrible, Muireall? Are you regretting our time together? Are you ashamed of me?"

She jumped up from her chair. "Of course I am not ashamed of you," she said and turned to stare out the window. "However, no one knows better than I that there are always consequences. Always."

He walked to her and picked up her hand. "Come and sit down. Try and relax. We are adults. There was no coercion."

Lucinda came in carrying the tea tray and seated herself. "Here we are. What do you like in your tea, Captain?"

"Mrs. Thompson, what you saw was my fault entirely. Miss Thompson is blameless," Anthony said.

"For a peck on the cheek? Just sugar for you, Muireall?"

"It was more than a peck on the cheek," Muireall said and sat down on the sofa. Anthony sat beside her.

Lucinda eyed them both. "I am no debutante. What you two choose to do or not do is not my business. Now. Let us get on to one of the reasons I stopped by."

Muireall closed her eyes. She was rarely if ever visibly angry or upset—there'd always been too many issues and people relying on her to be frivolous or dramatic. She was the eldest child of an earl and his countess, there was never meant to be self-serving tantrums or pity from anyone. She had duties to perform, and hysterics were not part of it.

"Yes, of course, please do continue, Lucinda." She took a deep breath and nodded politely.

Lucinda looked at her with the ghost of a smile hovering. But Lucinda had also been raised a lady and would never cause anyone undue discomfort or embarrassment. Lucinda looked at Anthony with a nod, and Muireall realized she could never again think of him as Mr. Marcus, not after recalling his naked body stretched out over hers. She felt herself blush.

"Actually, as I said before, I had intended to give a message to Muireall to give to you," Lucinda said.

"For me? What message could be for me, Mrs. Thompson?"

"It's from my father. His man of business, Mr. Critchfeld, is retiring."

"Yes, I met him briefly when we dined at your house."

"My father has been looking for a replacement for Mr. Critchfeld ever since he told him he was retiring nearly six months ago. He has considered candidates from all over the United States, and several foreign countries too, but has not found anyone he believes would suit the position."

"I can understand why it would be a very challenging job from what your father described to me that night. Manufacturing. Investments. Foreign governments. It would be extremely complicated, I think. And my first impression of your father was of a man who is focused and brilliant . . . and also convinced of his own rightness."

"How diplomatic you are." Lucinda smiled. "That is a very accurate assessment. A man who is not confident and clever as well would never be able to stand up to him and all his . . . rightness. Mr. Critchfeld was a master, although looking at him, one would never guess it."

Anthony glanced at Muireall and cocked his head to one side as he looked back at Lucinda. "I'm still not sure what the message is you were to give me."

"My father would like you to come meet with him. He thinks you may be the man who can carry on after Mr. Critchfeld."

"Excuse me?"

"He'd like to interview you as Mr. Critchfeld's replacement."

Anthony's eyes were wide, and he pushed back against his seat. "Interview me? I've recently been hired for a new position."

"Surely you could go hear what Lucinda's father has to say," Muireall said, her heart racing. She was certain that Henri Vermeal compensated his employees well, even if he was an exacting employer.

"With Endernoff Industries?" Lucinda asked.

"Yes. Mr. Endernoff offered me a position that should begin late January," he said. "Although it is not exactly the job that was advertised on the handbills."

"What did the handbills say?" Muireall asked.

"That it was a position overseeing one of his warehouses. After I'd met with him and he explained things further, I realized I would be loading and unloading crates from wagons and other conveyances."

Muireall glanced at him, thinking that his leg would pain him constantly, that he may even be unable to do the job. "That is why you've been hauling for the grocers and merchants in your neighborhood. You've been trying to strengthen your leg."

Anthony said nothing, just sipped at his tea, now certainly cold.

"Please, won't you say you'll come meet him? I think you will find him and his businesses a fascinating prospect. This position is salaried very generously."

He sat his cup down on the side table and leaned forward. "I don't want to be rude or ungrateful, but I don't want an opportunity like this offered to me only because I've become associated with the Thompson family."

Lucinda smiled. "You clearly underestimate my father. If he did not find you a compelling person, he would have never asked you to join him for a drink that evening or asked me to move the two of you to his table for dinner. He would have been coolly polite, as he generally is, but something about you, not the Thompsons, drove him to consider you. He is a complex man. Hard in business but with an uncanny eye to what he considers his greatest business asset: his people."

Muireall had never heard Lucinda speak in such a way. She was all business in a pretty, feminine, and very stylish dress. She imagined her sister-in-law was much like her father. She looked at Anthony. She was silently begging him to go to the interview. What an opportunity!

CHAPTER 7

Anthony Marcus did what he rarely did these days. He stopped in a tavern around the corner from his room after checking with the sisters that Ann was learning how to knit with the rest of the girls in the orphanage. He'd be buying her skeins of yarn in every color the next time he had a spare penny, he imagined with a chuckle. He pulled open the tavern door, the warmth hitting him in the face after the cold walk from Locust Street. The tables were filled with working men, some eating, mostly just drinking the local beer or whiskey. No one commented as he hobbled over to the bar, relying heavily on his cane.

"Whiskey, please. And a beer," he said to the woman behind the bar.

He threw back the glass of whiskey in one swallow, feeling its burn down his throat, closing his eyes, waiting for his mind to quiet after the tumultuous day. He supposed he'd be a fool to not at least speak to Mr. Vermeal. What could it hurt? He'd have to clean his suit again, polish his boots, and ask Mrs. Phillips to launder and press his good shirt. The time had been arranged before he'd left Muireall's home for day after next. He admitted to himself he was feeling nervous. Did that mean he wanted that job? Did he wonder what Muireall would think if he landed that job and had the courage to tell Mr. Endernoff, the only man in Philadelphia, up until this day, willing to take a chance on him? Yes, he most certainly did wonder.

He turned away from the barmaid, who was not Muireall Thompson, and stared blankly at a crookedly hung painting of a street of homes. She'd been naked with him. Dear God, he thought, looking around quickly as if he'd spoken aloud, aroused by the thought of it. He silently congratulated himself on managing to give her pleasure, as he was certain he had, instead of going off in her after one short minute. It had been years—three, he thought—since he'd been with a woman. He would have walked with a swagger had he not been leaning on his cane so heavily when he left Locust Street.

Could he support a wife on what he would make at Endernoff's? He wasn't quite sure, and certainly not in the style Muireall Thompson was accustomed to. Was he ready to make a commitment to a woman again? Of course he was ready. He'd already made that commitment when he'd been intimate with her, whether his mind recognized that at the time or not.

Muireall was certainly nothing like Virginia, his first wife and Ann's mother. The two women were opposite in every way and Ann would be thrilled if she could have Muireall in her daily life. He would have a little dream and a vivid memory, though, to enjoy for the coming weeks with the hope that memory would be repeated regularly.

HE REFUSED TO BE NERVOUS. AFTER ALL, HE HAD A JOB WITH Endernoff—not a great job, not even one he necessarily wanted, but a job all the same. He would make enough there to move to larger rooms. In fact, Mrs. Phillips had a set of rooms for let on the first floor with two bedrooms and a separate kitchen and living area. It would be perfect for he and Ann, and the price was not very much more than he was spending now, though currently more than he could pay.

He went to the orphanage once he was dressed to get a kiss from Ann before the Vermeal coach picked him up. He didn't expect to find Muireall Thompson there.

"Papa! You look very handsome!" Ann said after running to him and hugging him around the waist.

He chuckled. "A compliment from my favorite girl! I'll be home in a thrice. I don't imagine this meeting will take very long."

"It's all right, Papa. Miss Thompson is here, and she told me she plans to stay all afternoon."

"Did she?" He looked up to find her in the hallway. "Miss Thompson."

"Ann, would you mind helping Eliza with her reading."

"Good luck, Papa! I love you!" she shouted over her shoulder as she hurried back to the orphanage classroom.

"This isn't your usual day, is it?" he asked her.

"I wanted to tell you good luck." She glanced left and right and hurried across to him, planting a soft kiss on his cheek. "You will do very well, I think."

He smiled at her, wishing he could pull her into his arms. "Thank you. For that kiss and for your hope for my success."

She looked up at him, her face serious and determined. "You are a very special person. Deserving of a chance like this, although your success with your daughter is more important than anything else you may achieve. Good luck, Anthony," she whispered and patted his lapel.

He caught her hand and kissed her fingertips. "Thank you, Muireall. I will do my best."

She smiled at that comment and turned to the classroom. He would miss her at some point in his life. When she married someone else—he really must convince her he had not been trapped, when work or life took him away from Philadelphia. He was letting his mind get away from the rational to dark thoughts! He hurried outside, not wishing to be late.

The coach sent for him was opulent with uniformed staff as coachmen. He settled into the seat, hot bricks on the floor making his ride comfortable for his trip across town to the Vermeal mansion. He glanced out the window as they rode through gates on a graveled drive to the front door of the massive home. He navigated the steps, his cane clattering on the marble, to the door, which opened immediately.

He stepped inside, removed his hat and topcoat, and handed it to the butler. "Mr. Marcus to see Mr. Vermeal," he said.

"Yes, sir. Follow me," he said after handing off his wraps to another servant.

Anthony was shown into a room dominated by a desk and glass-fronted cabinets behind it. There was a fire burning brightly on the other side of the room, and the ten-foot-tall windows illuminated the thick dark carpet and its floral design.

"Ah, Captain. Have you eaten? I thought we could have some luncheon first."

"I haven't, Mr. Vermeal. Thank you."

The doors opened, and the butler came in with a cart—how he knew it was time for the meal Anthony did not know, but he appreciated the steaming aroma coming from the platters. He seated himself at the small table and shook out the linen napkin onto his lap. Vermeal was watching him, and it occurred to Anthony that everything would be a test today; every detail, including his table manners, would be examined.

"Are you a Philadelphia native, Captain?"

"No. My family is from New York, outside of Albany. My parents passed away when I and my sister were young, and we were raised after that by my father's parents. We were very fortunate. There was never any suggestion that we'd go to an orphanage or be fostered somewhere separately. Our grandparents and my uncle and his wife gladly saw to our upbringing and schooling. We had tutors at home, and I passed the exams to attend Union College in Schenectady and graduated in 1860. I joined the army as an officer, a second lieutenant, courtesy of my uncle's connections."

Their conversation veered then from the personal, including some of Vermeal's life history, to American and European current affairs. Anthony admitted to himself that it was a thoroughly enjoyable meal and that Vermeal was a fascinating man. Soon after a delicious lemon curd pudding, Mr. Critchfeld joined them.

"Won't you give our guest a rundown of what your day is like? I'm off to dictate a few letters to the secretary," Vermeal said, leaving the two men alone.

Critchfeld poured himself a cup of coffee from the tray nearby and sat down on a leather sofa near the fireplace. Anthony joined him.

"I thought I'd tell you how my days are generally spent," Critchfeld said and began a list of duties that Anthony could barely imagine, including contacting high-ranking officials in government, meeting inventors and businesspeople looking for investors, and the supervision of twenty office staff members. He was fascinated.

"How do you keep it all straight? All the appointments and projects?" Anthony asked.

"I have two secretaries that I use exclusively, and of course, if Mr. Vermeal determines he is interested in investing, I've several more staff members to assign tasks. There is also travel, which I will miss."

"Travel?" Anthony could hear the longing in his voice, and Critchfeld chuckled.

"We visit all our manufacturers every so often besides receiving monthly reports. Mr. Vermeal is generous and has allowed my wife to travel with me on several occasions. And I've bought stock in his public companies over the years, so I'm personally invested in guarding our profits." He looked at

Anthony with a small smile. "I've accumulated considerable wealth from the investments as well as receiving a substantial salary. I'll retire a wealthy man, nothing like Vermeal, of course, but more than happy with my situation with substantial inheritances for each of my nine children."

"Nine children?"

Critchfeld smiled. "It seems like Nellie came home from our travels expecting another child more often than not."

Anthony laughed, liking this man more than he'd expected to and respecting him as well. "What is Mr. Vermeal like to work for?"

Critchfeld settled back on the sofa and placed his empty coffee cup on the side table. "He and I disagree occasionally, although we mostly are of the same mind on general discussions. He never denigrates. He's always respectful and listens to my reasoning. He doesn't always follow it, but he has followed my advice sometimes. I've been mostly right, but when I wasn't, he shrugged it off and said we were to move on. He understands that business decisions are made with the best information we can obtain, through the lens of experience, with the most qualified staff we can assemble, but there is still some luck and intuition involved. That's not to say he doesn't make his displeasure known. It's just not personal unless it involves his daughter or sister. And then he is a bear!"

Anthony laughed. "I got the impression that he is not fond of Mr. Thompson."

"You have no idea," he said, shaking his head. "But Miss Lucinda is cut from the same cloth, and he is grooming her to take over the company. Quite unusual for a woman to be trusted in that way, but she is astute and extremely bright. She'll be the next generation of Vermeal Industries, that's for certain. Could you work for a woman?"

"I thought that was what our jobs were all along, to work for women."

Critchfeld laughed outright. "There's no doubt Nellie runs the ship in our family! But you will have to consider that if he offers you this position. In ten years, Mrs. Thompson will likely be running this company, and she will need a loyal and experienced second-in-command, especially during the first few years."

Critchfeld was staring at him, waiting for a reply, and Anthony felt as if his response would be weighty in the decision to offer him the position or not. He could do nothing other than tell the truth.

"I've known loyalty since I was a child, first from my parent's upbringing of my sister and I, to our acceptance and love from our grandparents. I found the military to my liking to some degree because I felt I could rely on my fellow officers and soldiers, that I would have their back and they would have mine. I don't have to lead every charge, but I appreciate my opinion being respected. To work for a company that values those things would be very rewarding, I believe."

"Well," Critchfeld said and stood to shake his hand. "Let me get Mr. Vermeal. You've passed my tests."

"Thank you, sir."

Mr. Vermeal returned shortly carrying two thick green leather folders. He handed them both to Anthony.

"Read as much as you can about each company. There's a two-page summary on the top. Tell me which company Vermeal Industries should invest in. I'll be back in an hour."

Anthony sat down at the desk, opening the first folder and finding a pencil and a stack of clean white paper, which he was more envious of than any part of this admittedly magnificent dwelling. To have a stack of paper like this when teaching Ann her numbers and letters would have been a luxury indeed.

He quickly put aside his fanciful thoughts and concentrated on the detailed summary of Company A. When Mr. Vermeal came back in the room, Anthony was standing, the portfolios stacked neatly on the corner of the desk beside him. Mr. Vermeal glanced at the folders and back to his face.

"What are your conclusions, Mr. Marcus?"

"I believe you recently purchased Company B, sir. I read about LeFeat's a few weeks ago in the *Inquirer*, and this portfolio puts me in mind of them, down to the last detail. The paper said an international company based in Philadelphia with worldwide holdings had won the bidding war. That the negotiations were led in part by the owner's daughter, certainly unique in today's business world."

"And Company A?"

"I would suggest you stay away from that company, sir, if you already haven't. I'm no expert, but the balance sheets smell of fraud."

Vermeal held out his hand in a quick dismissal, and Anthony stepped forward to shake his hand. Perhaps he'd been too forward. Perhaps Mr. Vermeal did not want that type of summary.

"It's been a pleasure meeting with you, Mr. Marcus. I'll be forwarding my answer within the next day or two. Laurent will see you out," he said. The door opened, as if by magic, to reveal the butler in the hallway, holding Anthony's coat and hat.

"Thank you for the lunch, Mr. Vermeal, and for the interesting conversation," he said and walked to the door. It had been interesting, he thought as the butler helped him on with his coat. He led him to the front door, where the Vermeal carriage awaited.

"Thank you," he said as the man held the door.

"A pleasure, sir. We hope to see you again."

Anthony glanced at him, wondering if he said that to every one of Vermeal's guests, but the butler's face showed not an inkling of welcome or rebuke. The perfect servant's countenance.

. . .

Muireall came out of the orphanage door just as Mr. Bauer pulled up in James's carriage, the horses prancing and blowing steam in the frigid air.

"How are you today, Miss Thompson? How are the children?" Mr. Bauer asked after climbing down from his perch.

"The children are wonderfully active, and I am exhausted. Hopefully, Mrs. McClintok has dinner well under control."

Mr. Bauer chuckled as he handed her inside the carriage. She plopped down onto the cushioned seat with a sigh. She had not heard from Anthony in nearly a week, although she'd seen Ann several times at the orphanage. She said her Papa was again delivering groceries to elderly customers of the neighborhood grocer. Philadelphia had been in a freeze with high winds for the last several days, and she worried about him slipping on the ice that was everywhere. Ann said he'd broken out his army topcoat to wear in the frigid weather and had been carrying her the half block to the orphanage wrapped in a blanket.

Mr. Bauer escorted her up the steps on Locust Street, hanging on to his arm as her boots slipped on the ice with each step. She did not understand how the coachman could manage to stay upright. "Would you and Mr. Jenson like to come inside for a warm drink?"

"No, thank you, ma'am. We'll be getting the horses stabled out of this wind, and Mrs. Howell, your brother's housekeeper, will have hot coffee for us. But thank you."

Muireall slipped inside, struggling to pull the door shut against the wind. Mrs. McClintok hurried down the hallway.

"Let me take your coat; the hem is soaked."

"Thank you. It is bitter outside. Did the coal delivery arrive? I've had a note from James that Aunt Murdoch will be staying with them until this cold snap passes. Perhaps we should check on Mrs. Mingo down the street and make sure she has wood for her stove."

"The coal was delivered this morning shortly after you left. I sent Robbie down to Mrs. Mingo's yesterday with a pot of soup and a loaf of your bread. He filled her woodstove and carried in a pile from outside. I told him he'll have to check on her every other day or so."

"Tell him to stuff rugs under her doors and rags around her windows. The last time I was there, the air was blowing in as if the sash were open." Muireall handed Mrs. McClintok her scarf.

A knock sounded and Mrs. McClintok opened the door. "Oh, Mr. Marcus. Do come in out of the cold!"

Muireall smiled. She couldn't help herself. She was just so glad to see him, even if his ears and cheeks were bright red from the cold. "Certainly, you haven't walked the whole way here from Devlin Street?"

He smiled in return as he unwrapped a dark blue scarf from his neck and unbuttoned a knee-length military overcoat. Mrs. McClintok took it from him as he shrugged it off his shoulders.

"Goodness, this is heavy. All wool, I suspect," she said. "I'm going to hang it in the kitchen near the stove so it dries."

"Won't you come in and warm yourself near the fire? I'm sure Mrs. McClintok will be bringing us coffee and cake very soon as I've just come home from the orphanage myself."

"I would appreciate that very much," he said and indicated her to lead the way.

Muireall sat down on the sofa, hoping he'd sit with her rather than in one of the chairs. She was rewarded when he sat beside her, his trousers touching her skirts. He picked up her hand and looked at her with a small smile.

"What is it?" she asked, searching his face.

Mrs. McClintok made some noise as she approached the sitting room door and again when opening it. Muireall was not thrilled that there was speculation about her relationship with Anthony, but she did appreciate the chance to jump apart if necessary. Anthony, however, did not move away or release her hand.

"Here is some nice hot coffee and cinnamon-and-walnut cake with butter icing," Mrs. McClintok said as she rolled the cart to Muireall's side. Muireall thanked her and set about pouring their coffee and putting slices of cake on the small plates. She picked up the cup and saucer, a linen napkin, and turned to him.

"Not yet, Muireall. I've got to tell you something first," he said.

"All right," she said and set the coffee down on the cart. "What is it, Anthony?"

"Mr. Vermeal has offered me the position as his assistant."

Her hands flew to cover her mouth. "Oh, Anthony! Congratulations!" She did not know who instigated the embrace, but she was in his arms then, hugging him tightly.

He leaned back to look her in the eye. "Mr. Vermeal said I should take a day or two to think about the offer, talk to my family, and let him know my decision." He laid his hand on her cheek. "Only two people came to mind that I must discuss this opportunity with. Ann and you."

She held both of his hands. "I am honored. I admit I have been worrying, but it was for naught. Mr. Vermeal saw you for who you are. I am so very happy for you and Ann."

"Are you happy for us?" he said and lifted her chin with his forefinger.

"Well," she said and licked her lips. "Is there an *us*, Anthony?"

"There is an us when I want to share my news with you above all. There's an us when you're worried for me." He kissed her lips softly, brushing his back and forth over hers. "There was an us when we were together upstairs. When we made love."

Her eyes fluttered. She was no green girl, but she could not deny feeling giddy, as if she could dance a jig at that moment. As if all was right with the world. As if there was nothing that could stop them. But she must be realistic. She'd always been, and it served her well as she charted her family's course since she was fourteen.

"Tell me everything, Anthony." She released his hands to pick up his coffee and offer it to him.

He took a sip and held the cup on his knee. "The salary is unbelievable, Muireall. May I tell you the amount? Would that be gauche?"

"Not when it is just us, and only if you are comfortable telling me."

"One thousand dollars a month," he said and shook his head in disbelief. "One thousand dollars a month."

"Oh, Anthony! You will be able to rent a larger house for you and Ann."

"That won't even be necessary, Muireall. He is installing me in a house he owns, complete with staff and a carriage. It is in addition to the salary. It is close to his home, so it's for his convenience too."

"You deserve this and more, Anthony. I am so very happy for you."

"I can hardly believe it."

"I can believe it. No one is more worthy."

CHAPTER 8

"I promise, Mrs. Phillips. I will not forget to stop and see you," Anthony said to his landlady as the last of his things were loaded into a closed wagon sent by his stableman, Mr. Reynolds, to Devlin Street. *His stableman!* It was still hard to believe that the changes in his life were real. That they'd actually happened.

"I'm so happy for you and that dear child of yours," she said as she wiped tears from her eyes.

"And do not hesitate to call on John Pennyknoll. He's a good all-around carpenter and won't gouge you. And the veterans, especially the wounded ones, need work."

"Mr. Pennyknoll seems to know his way around a hammer, but it won't be you."

"You are too kind. Now please get out of this wind. I carried down all the extra coal I had in my rooms for you to use."

He looked over her shoulder and saw Ann trudging through the snow holding the hand of Sister Ann Marie. She was not chattering or smiling. In fact, her head was hanging. Strange to see his girl less than happy, especially as of late, after he'd told her about having her own room and a school nearby her new home for her to attend. She looked up, saw him, and ran straight to him. Her face was tear streaked.

"Papa," she said softly against his neck as he held her. "I will miss the sisters and all the children. I want to take them all with us to our new home so they will have a home too, but I know I can't."

He kissed her forehead. "I've promised Mrs. Phillips we will visit occasionally. We'll make time to visit the orphanage too."

"Maybe Miss Thompson will bring me with her when she comes."

"We will see."

"I'm excited about all the changes and scared too, Papa."

"I know exactly what you mean. It is a bit overwhelming."

She shimmied down from his arms and hurried over to hug Mrs. Phillips, who was drying her tears with the corner of her white apron. Anthony glanced up at the windows of his room, his former room, and felt a little melancholy too. Not for the worry that he wouldn't be able to pay Mrs. Phillips what was owed or if he would be able to replace Ann's clothes as she grew out of them, but for the community that he'd found in the orphanage, at the grocer and other businesses, and with his landlady.

He would not be sad long, however, and he did not think Ann would be either. Not once they'd settled into their new home on Spruce and 33rd Street. The street bordered the wealthiest section of the city and was only a few blocks from the Vermeal mansion and their headquarters nearby. He'd been to see it already, accompanied by Mr. Critchfeld and the housekeeper, Mrs. Smithy, who was to see to the redecorating or updating that would need to be done. He'd been overwhelmed at the time and said very little. The house held fifteen rooms, not counting staff quarters. There was a small ballroom, a large library, a formal dining room, and a casual parlor on the second floor where he imagined he and Ann would spend much of their time. There was indoor plumbing, including hot water and a bathing room near his suite and one on the top floor for the staff. The kitchen, which the cook informed him she would prefer he stay out of, had every modern appliance available recently installed.

He took Ann's hand as she waved with the other to Mrs. Phillips and led her to the small carriage, where Reynolds was holding open the door for he and Ann to climb in. He turned to her when they were settled and she'd shouted her last good-bye to Mrs. Phillips. Reynolds climbed in his seat in front of them, flicking the reins for the horse to begin moving.

"We are on our way, Papa," she said. "There are so many things to think about!"

"We are on our way, but we are not going to hurry any of our decisions. We are going to take our time and allow ourselves to be accustomed to our new home. Other than new clothes I've ordered and the new clothes to be made for you, we need not worry about anything."

"Yes, Papa."

Twenty minutes later, she was latched on to his arm as they pulled up to the brick house, the snow swept from the stone walkway and steps. They both sat still, looking at the bright red front door and peering up at the three stories of windows, even after Reynolds had opened the door of the carriage.

"Come along now, dear," he said. "Let us see our new lodgings."

She glanced at him. "It seems every bit as nice as Mrs. Phillips's house."

It took him a moment to realize she was teasing him, trying to lighten their mood. "I will miss the steps that creaked so loudly I worried I was about to fall through them."

"I will miss running to the water closet in the middle of a cold night," she said with a smile.

"Perhaps we will tell the housekeeper to light no fires in our sleeping rooms so we will be comfortably cold."

She laughed then and looked back at the house through the

open carriage door. "Oh, Papa! It is so beautiful! And we are keeping poor Mr. Reynolds out in the cold."

She held his hand as they went up the brick walk. The door was opened by Mrs. Smithy. "Come in out of this weather, young lady," the woman said.

"It is very cold out," Ann said and held out her hand. "Good morning. I am Ann Marcus."

The housekeeper smiled and took her hand. "And I am Mrs. Smithy. I am so glad to be managing a household with such a lovely young lady in residence." She looked up at him. "Welcome home, sir."

A young maid took their coats and hurried away without a word. "That is Sarah. She's terribly shy but an excellent worker."

"I'm sure she is, Mrs. Smithy. Mr. Critchfeld assured me your judgment is impeccable."

The housekeeper smiled, and Anthony hoped his words and tone would be the beginning of a smooth transition, especially knowing that Mrs. Smithy would be very involved with Ann's life. He anticipated very long days as he learned his new position, and there would be evenings where he would be required to attend entertainments and dinners. His recent employment was both terrifying and daunting and the most interesting and exciting thing that had ever happened to him. He must write his sister and aunt and uncle with the news.

"THERE'S A MESSAGE FOR YOU, MISS THOMPSON," MRS. McClintok said to her as she came down the steps from her room. It was already eight in the morning, and she'd just climbed out of bed, even then groggy and tired. Payden had spent the day before with a handkerchief by his nose, and she thought he might have passed on his illness to her. She took the note from Mrs. McClintok's hand.

Miss Thompson,

It is long past time that Ann has new dresses and shoes. Could you recommend a dressmaker who fashions clothes for a young girl?

Yours,

Anthony Marcus

"Would you ask Robbie to take a message to Mr. Marcus, please? Give him coins for the trolley. It is too far on foot."

"Yes, ma'am. He and Master Payden are out clearing walkways for some of the elderly on the block. They will both go, I imagine."

Muireall wrote a quick note and returned to the kitchen to give it to the housekeeper. "Ah, Mr. Bamblebit. It's good to see you," she said to the gentleman standing very close to Mrs. McClintok, who turned to the stove, stirring whatever was in the huge pot.

"Miss Thompson," he said.

"It looks as though this bitter weather is about to break, does it not?"

"It does," he replied and took the note from her hand. "I was leaving shortly and know where the boys are shoveling. I'll deliver it to them."

"Thank you," she said.

He turned to Mrs. McClintok. "I'll see you Saturday at four, then."

She nodded, and he went to the door.

"Another outing?" Muireall asked with a smile. "He's very attentive."

"He is. He's also steady and hardworking," she said and glanced at Muireall. "And very handsome."

Muireall thought the thickly built and dark-haired man rather grim, as she'd never seen him smile. He had a thin white scar down one cheek, and his nose was wide, as if he'd survived several punches to the face, which was most likely true as he worked for her brother-in-law Alexander's family in security. But he seemed increasingly devoted to the Thompson housekeeper.

Muireall smiled. "Handsome is always a wonderful addition to any suitor."

"Like Mr. Marcus?" she replied, a grin on her face.

"Yes. Like Mr. Marcus," she said and looked closely at her. "Should I be looking for a new housekeeper?"

The woman shook her head. "Nay. I've already told him—well, rather hinted to him—that I wouldn't be making any changes to my life until my Robbie is grown and on his way."

"Hinted?"

"He told me the second time we stepped out together that he would marry me the next day. That he owns a small house, paid for, where he lives with an elderly aunt who had nowhere to go when her daughter, his cousin, passed away. He told me he wasn't looking for someone to tend the aunt but that he recognized . . . that he knew that I was the woman he'd been looking for all of his life."

Muireall's eyes filled with tears, and she had no idea why. "Oh, how perfectly lovely. Robbie will be a grown man in a few short years, so I doubt your wait will be overly long. If that is what you want, of course. You know you will have a home with us for as long as you need."

"Robbie and I have been blessed to be part of this household, Muireall. You know I would never leave you in a lurch."

Muireall walked to her and held her shoulders. "Of course I know that. But sometimes life has surprises for us. Good surprises."

"Like Mr. Marcus."

"Like Mr. Bamblebit."

MUIREALL HURRIED DOWN THE STEPS AND PULLED ON HER heavy coat. She'd slept late again and had to hurry to ready herself and was just pinning on her hat when Mrs. McClintok knocked on her bedroom door to tell her that her sister had arrived. They were picking up Ann Marcus in a short time and meeting their sister Kirsty at her fabric shop.

"Thank you, Mrs. McClintok! I should be home later this afternoon depending on how long we are at the dressmakers."

Muireall stepped out the door, looking forward to the outing, and climbed in the Pendergast carriage beside her sister with the help of their coachman.

"I cannot tell you how glad I am that you asked me to join you to order Ann new clothes," Elspeth said. "With this terrible weather, I needed something to look forward to."

"Agreed. Pretty plaids and prints and ruffles and bows instead of ice and snow," Muireall said.

"I've been clamoring for a reason to venture out, and you presented me with the perfect excuse."

"How is Jonathon?"

Elspeth smiled. "He is sitting up by himself and rolling over when left to his own devices on a blanket. Alexander is thrilled I am going out and told me that he will be spending the day with his son as I never allow him any long periods alone with him. My husband is unreasonably dear when it comes to Jonathon."

Muireall watched her sister, glad in her heart that Elspeth had lived through her dangerous ordeal and was well enough afterward to find love and happiness. She did not think that Elspeth was covering up sadness, although who really knew how deep her scars were, but she knew her sister fought for her happiness and that she was more than just content with her life with Alexander and little Jonathon.

The carriage pulled up to Mr. Marcus's new home, the first Muireall had seen it, a beautiful three-story brick with wide tall windows and a welcoming look. The door opened at that moment, and Anthony and Ann began down the walk. He was holding her hand with his free one, probably to keep her from charging to the carriage and jumping inside, and she looked excited enough to do just that. Anthony waved off the coachman and opened the door. Ann climbed in with his help.

"Mrs. Pendergast," he said, nodded, and turned to Muireall. "Miss Thompson. You are looking particularly well today. I can't thank you enough for tending to this chore for me. I would have no idea what a young girl would need other than the basics."

"Chore? Shopping is not a chore, Mr. Marcus. My sisters and I will enjoy ourselves immensely as we have a lovely young lady to outfit."

"Have the dressmaker send the bill here, and please make sure to include a winter coat in the purchases," he said.

"I do not want a new coat if it will not match my mittens and scarf," Ann said, looking at her father defiantly.

"We will make sure that we choose fabric that will complement both," Muireall said. "There will be many fabrics to choose from in all different shades. I'm hoping that we will find a nice plaid for a coat for you and surely one that will match your scarf and mittens."

"More than one to choose from?" she asked.

Elspeth picked up Ann's hand and held it fast in her own. "So many we won't know what to choose!"

"Oh," she said with a smile and turned to her father. "We will be back soon, Papa. Please close the carriage door."

Elspeth laughed, and Muireall smiled at Anthony. He leaned to her when Elspeth engaged Ann in conversation. "Mr. Vermeal has allocated money for moving expenses to me, although I certainly didn't incur any as the staff here moved our belongings, not that there was that much to see to. Get her what she needs and a thing or two she may want, even if it is frivolous. Thank you," he said softly. "Muireall."

"You're welcome, Anthony," she whispered. They looked into each other's eyes, and she felt a connection to him, certainly more than an acquaintance or a friend. She believed she wanted to spend every day with him, even knowing that there would be days she would be frustrated and angry with him, as any couple would do, which was so different from her single state. She was starting to wonder if she loved him. Wonder? she thought to herself. She was very much in love with him. She would have never climbed naked into a bed with him if she wasn't.

"Papa! Please close the carriage door. We have an appointment, you see, and should not be late," Ann said.

Anthony smiled. "Of course, ladies. I do not want to keep you from your shopping."

Elspeth was still laughing as the carriage rolled down the street toward Kirsty's shop. Her youngest sister climbed in and sat down on the other side of Ann after she'd given the coachman directions to The Rose Dress Shoppe.

"Miss Buchman specializes in young ladies' clothing. She carries many of my fabrics, and if there's something she doesn't stock, then we will look in my back room, but I think we will find everything you could want at her shop. Ronda is particularly good at matching flattering styles and color to a client, even a very young client."

"My Papa said I was to have everything I need. I'm to start school soon," she said.

"And you will have everything you need, miss, as we will be gladly spending your father's money." Kirsty smiled.

Ann shook her head. "Oh no. We mustn't buy too much. We must be careful with our money."

"I've spoken to your father about that, Ann. He is adamant that you have everything you need. Let your father and I worry about the bill, and you enjoy yourself," Muireall said, just then glancing at her sisters, who both looked at her with raised brows. She sounded much too proprietary, and they had both heard it in her voice.

"Yes, ma'am," Ann said. "It is hard not to worry, though."

"Here we are!" Kirsty said.

Several hours later, Muireall directed the coachman to take

them to Foster's Tea Room for their luncheon. Muireall took Ann by the hand to the ladies' retiring room when they arrived to wash her hands and face while Elspeth and Kirsty were seated.

"Oh, Miss Thompson! I am so excited about all my new things I could burst. And now we are to eat in a restaurant! Wait until I tell Papa!"

"We had a very successful day at Miss Buchman's, and I thought we could all use a meal. We must be mindful of our manners. The dining room is quite full."

Ann looked up at her. "I will do my best, ma'am."

"I'm sure you will," Muireall said and bent to kiss the girl's cheek. Ann wrapped her arms around Muireall's waist, burying her face in Muireall's coat.

"I had such a wonderful day. I am very lucky to have such a good Papa, but it was very nice to spend the day with ladies. Do not tell him, please. I don't want him to be upset."

"Your father would never begrudge you a pleasure. He only wants your happiness."

She glanced up, her eyes sparkling with mischief. "Then I will tell him all about the fancy desserts Mrs. Watson described."

"Absolutely!" she said, cupping Ann's face in her hand. "Let us go eat until we cannot squeeze in another morsel!"

CHAPTER 9

Anthony rightly thought at the time the massive job of winding down a war, finding families of the fallen, paying the last stipend soldiers were owed, unmanning the war offices, and informing officers that their future was as a civilian, was challenging at every decision. But beginning his work with Vermeal Industries was ten times the challenge, maybe one hundred times more difficult, and certainly more exciting. His respect for Critchfeld increased daily. The man was a wizard at anticipating and finding the information or expert that Vermeal would need prior to being asked.

The job required the second-in-command to be fully knowledgeable of every avenue Vermeal was studying. Some of it was purely years of practice, understanding what questions would need to be answered prior to any decision being made, but some of it was instinct, which Critchfeld had in abundance. Anthony hoped that he would be up to the challenge. He was certainly going to try. He had quickly become accustomed to having cooked meals and sparkling white sheets on his bed and someone to take care of his and Ann's clothing. Mrs. Smithy met him at the door every evening to take his new wool topcoat and his leather case that held his evening's reading.

Ann seemed to be adjusting well, although she often mentioned the sisters and Mrs. Phillips. She was still overwhelmed, he thought, and although she was thrilled having her own bedroom with pink ruffled curtains and bedclothes, thick carpet, and tall windows, filling the room with light, she clung to him when he was home. They'd spent the last several years in each other's pockets, and now his long workdays and a home with multiple rooms kept them separated.

"Papa! Papa!"

He stood from his desk in the small room he'd claimed as an office for himself, grabbing his cane and hurrying out the door to the top of the staircase. "Ann?"

"Here I am, Papa! Oh, thank you, Mrs. Smithy," she said as the housekeeper took her coat and hat. "I am home, and I have so much to tell you! Are you very busy?'

"Never too busy for you," he said and made his way down the curved staircase to the large marble tiled entryway. "Was the shopping successful?"

"Oh yes. Miss Buchman was most helpful and had a few things already made that I could bring home today. Mr. Reynolds is carrying in some packages right now I must show you!"

"Can I offer you coffee, Miss Thompson? Mrs. Pendergast?" he said, smiling and turning in the direction of the sisters.

"Oh dear, no," Mrs. Pendergast said. "We've just come from Foster's and drank pots of tea."

"And the desserts! We must go, just the two of us, or you could ask Miss Thompson to come with us. The desserts were wonderful!"

Anthony glanced at Muireall, who was smiling at him. He turned to his daughter. "Perhaps you and Mrs. Smithy could take your purchases to your room after you've thanked the ladies. I'll be there shortly to see everything."

Ann hugged Muireall around the waist, turned to Mrs. Pendergast, and held out her hand. "Thank you ever so much."

"I'll be in the carriage," Mrs. Pendergast said to her sister and turned to him. "Ann is a joy."

The front door closed finally, and he could only faintly hear Ann talking to Mrs. Smithy. They must be in her room. He looked at Muireall.

"I can't thank you enough for taking her."

"No thanks are necessary. I enjoyed myself immensely. Ann is well-behaved and so very clever. I love spending time with her."

He did what he wanted then. He walked toward her and pulled her into his arms. "She loves you, you know." Anthony watched her eyes fill with tears and shook his head. "I didn't mean to upset you, Muireall."

Her lip trembled. "I love her very much. She's not my daughter, though, and I don't want to presume."

Anthony held her cheeks in his hands and kissed her softly, saying the words that had circled in his head for weeks. "She could be, Muireall. She could be your daughter."

"You mustn't say such a thing," she said on a sob.

"Why not? Why should we be denied? I intend to save much of my income for several months, other than the necessities such as Ann's clothing purchased today. If necessary, we would be able to live modestly but comfortably if I lost this job and until I was employed again. I'm hoping to be in that position by midsummer. I will reopen this subject with you at that time."

"Oh, Anthony. What are you saying?"

"I'm saying I want to marry you. I want us to be a family. I want to have a wife and Ann to have a mother. More than anything, I want you to have a husband so you will have someone to rely on and you won't always have to be the one to worry and plan. I want to take some of your responsibilities from your shoulders and make them mine."

"I'm too old for marriage," she cried and sobbed in truth. "I'm old and set in my ways."

He pulled her into his arms and rubbed her back in slow

circles. "Muireall, darling, don't distress yourself. I never meant to overset you. There is nothing to think about now. Let me dry your tears." He pulled out his hankie, dried her face, and held it to her nose. She took it from his hands.

"I'm sorry, Anthony. I didn't mean to become emotional. I'm flattered and tempted." She looked up at him. "I just don't know what to think, which is very unusual for me."

"We've already been tempted and since this is my second poor attempt at flattery, you must have pity on me. But there is no need to think about anything right now. All we need to do is get you into your sister's carriage," he said and kissed her forehead.

"Muireall? Muireall? Are you well?"

Muireall rolled over and looked into her sister-in-law's face. "Lucinda? Whatever are you doing here so early? Is everything all right with the baby? James?"

Lucinda patted her stomach. "Other than this child keeping me awake at night with his rolling and pushing, I'm fine. My father and husband have lost their minds, however. I am to be swaddled for the next few months and do nothing more strenuous than drink my tea."

Muireall pulled herself up on her elbows. "What time is it?"

"Half past ten. Mrs. McClintok tried to wake you earlier, but—"

"Good Lord! I've slept the morning away, and I was planning on going to the orphanage." Muireall pushed back the covers and sat up on the side of the bed. "I'll be dressed in no time, and we can chat. If you'll just ask Mrs. McClintok to send up hot water."

But Lucinda did not leave the room. She pulled the ladder-back chair to the side of Muireall's bed and sat down. "Mrs. McClintok said you'd been sleeping late often. Are you feeling well, Muireall?"

"I've just been so very tired lately. I don't know what it is.

Maybe just pining for spring, like Aunt Murdoch," she said and made to stand. She dropped back down onto the bed. "Oh dear. I'm a bit dizzy. Maybe I am coming down with something." Lucinda stared at her for the longest time. "What? What are you thinking?"

"When was the last time you had your courses?"

"My courses? Whatever would that have to do with . . ." But then she knew what they would have to do with, and she knew they came on time every month. She jumped from the bed, held on to the footboard to keep her footing, and went to the small writing desk in the corner of her room where she kept track of everything from when she should inventory linens to her siblings' birthdays. She counted forward from the small check by a date on her calendar. "Three weeks late. I'm three weeks late."

"Five weeks since the time I stopped by to ask you to give a message to Mr. Marcus."

Muireall looked at her carved walnut headboard, at the pillows against it where his head had lain as he held her, at the small table beside her bed where his cane had rested. She must think. She must think! She looked at Lucinda. "Thank you for coming by today. I'm sorry I won't be able to join you for a chat."

Lucinda raised her brows and stood. "Of course, Muireall."

She spoke when Lucinda's hand was on the doorknob. "I'm hoping you can withhold this from James until I've made some decisions."

"My discretion is guaranteed," she said and then looked over her shoulder. "But you must tell Mr. Marcus as soon as possible."

Consequences, she thought. There were always consequences.

IT HAD TAKEN HER A FULL WEEK TO GET HER EMOTIONS AND thoughts under control. She avoided every mirror in the Locust Street house because otherwise she found herself turning sideways to see if there was any physical proof that she actually was expecting a child. Sometimes she went hours denying the entire thing because she was the sensible daughter of an earl and his countess and would not do something as shameful and stupid as be with child and unmarried. She would bear a bastard! That hideous thought brought tears to her eyes and self-recriminations to her heart. How reckless she'd been!

She did know that Lucinda was correct. She must tell Anthony. She had put it off long enough and had sent a note that very morning for him to please visit her at two in the afternoon, knowing that Mrs. McClintok would be doing the household shopping and that Payden and Robbie were both spending the afternoon with James at his gymnasium. She heard his knock, took a deep breath, and willed herself to tamp down the turmoil, the constant remorse, and the inexplicable sorrow.

"Mr. Marcus. Won't you come in?" she said after opening the door.

"I cannot tell you how glad I was to receive your note to stop by," he said, smiling as he pulled off his coat and gloves. "I have been missing you sorely!"

"I have tea ready unless you would prefer coffee." She turned to lead him down the hallway and through the open doors to the sitting room. He caught her arm as she stepped into the room.

"Muireall. What is it?"

She turned away from him and sat in her chair. "Shall I pour?"

He pulled her to her feet, kissed her cheek, and she felt tears threaten. She must maintain the calmness she'd worked so hard for.

"Muireall, love, what is troubling you?"

She seated herself and waited until he was seated across from her. "I'm sorry to have taken you away from you work, Mr. Marcus, but there is something quite important I must inform you of."

"What is this 'Mr. Marcus' nonsense? Am I no longer Anthony? Am I here for you to give me my marching orders?" He smiled, although it slowly faded when she did not respond to his teasing. "I am to be dismissed, then?"

Muireall took a sip of tea, placed the cup on the cart, and faced him, looking into his eyes, into the face that had become increasingly dear to her. To the face of the man she respected and loved.

"I'm expecting a child." Her eyelids fluttered and her lip trembled as those words were spoken. Words that could never be returned from whence they came. "Of course, I'll find a place to move to—"

Anthony sprang from his seat, smiling and laughing, and pulled her to her feet, swinging her around until her feet left the floor. "I've been hoping and praying that our lovemaking would have results! I love you, Muireall Thompson! I will make all the arrangements so we can marry right away."

"Put me down! Oh, please put me down!"

"What is it, love? We're to be a family! You have made me the happiest of men!"

She shook her head. "No, Anthony. You must not weave these fantastical scenes. You have a new and prestigious job—and a daughter. I have a brother to continue raising, an elderly aunt to care for, and a house to maintain."

He dropped his hands from her shoulders and stepped back from her. "What are you talking about, Muireall?"

"We both have commitments that we must see to."

"We made a commitment to *each other* that day in your room, Muireall. Did you not realize?"

She shook her head. "There was an attraction, which we satisfied, but there were consequences."

"An attraction? Muireall, we have made a child together. A son or daughter. We were not married, but—"

"We weren't married! Don't you see! I'm the eldest daughter of the Earl and Countess of Taviston! We do not produce bastard children!" she said as watched his face turn a frightening shade of white.

"I will not allow you to speak that way of a child. Our child. Our innocent child," he said through gritted teeth. "An earl? What are you talking about?"

Muireall dropped into her seat and took a deep breath. "My parents are, were, the Earl and Countess of Taviston. A Scottish title. Our home was Dunacres with over ten thousand acres and hundreds of tenants. My father's illegitimate cousin made a claim to the title and properties, and though his cause had no basis in Scottish law, dangerous things began to happen. Payden was kidnapped when he was but three or four months old. My mother was pushed down a set of steps and lost a child, nearly lost her life. My father set sail with all of us for America, including Aunt Murdoch, my mother's aunt, to keep us safe. He planned to return to Scotland once he had us settled to manage Dunacres and follow the cousin's suit in the Court of the Lord Lyon."

He was leaning forward, forearms on his knees, listening intently. "What happened?"

"Mother and Father were murdered on the voyage and were buried at sea. They were poisoned. We stayed together in one room for the rest of the journey. Murdoch went to the kitchens herself for food for us. We arrived in New York, reserved hotel rooms for a week, and slipped out in the middle of the first night to travel to Philadelphia."

"My God," he whispered.

"Murdoch and I found this house, moved us in, and began the change from the MacTavishes to the Thompsons. Father had told me as he lay dying where the gold he'd brought was hidden and about the bank accounts he'd already set up."

"How old were you?"

"Thirteen. Nearly fourteen. I had James, who is a first cousin, not a brother, Elspeth, who was nine, Kirsty five, and the new Lord Taviston, only one-year-old, my brother Payden, to raise and care for. Plowman—that is the illegitimate cousin—found us two years ago. His suit was in court for nearly twenty years, and it was clear he was losing. He decided the best thing to do was to get the earl, and that is what he has attempted with both Elspeth and Kirsty, hoping to ransom them for Payden. But they both know, we all know, we would never give him up."

"Good God, Muireall. I had no idea."

"Of course not. We don't share this story because there's still danger."

"What happened to your sisters?"

"Kirsty was nearly abducted, but Albert and James and Alexander arrived before they could take her, although Alexander suffered a gunshot wound. Albert hid her until the danger passed. Elspeth was kidnapped from Alexander's home during a ball and held for ransom."

"Dear Lord," he said, shocked. "All of this, as terrible as it is, does not explain why you won't marry me."

"I can't just up and marry. I have obligations. I committed my life to this family, to the Taviston legacy. You're asking me to give it all up! To turn my back on all those promises I made to my parents as they took their last breaths," she whispered as tears spilled onto her cheeks. "I can't do it."

He stood from the chair he sat on, wobbling a bit, as if unsure of himself in more ways than just a leg that wasn't reliable. He walked to the window, staring out and rubbing his forehead with his hand. Muireall watched him. His strong, straight back and military posture. She loved him. She was having his child and dying inside.

He turned slowly and stared at her. "What makes you believe that I would ever, ever come between you and your family? You think so little of me that you believe I would separate you from them? That I would not support you in any way I could? You do not understand love, I don't think." He pulled on his coat and went to the doorway. "I'll call on you in a week. Please discuss this with your family."

Muireall heard the front door close and felt her heart crack. Oh God. What had she done?

* * *

MUIREALL HAD SPENT THE FOLLOWING WEEK TRYING TO ADJUST herself to her pregnancy. She had no intention of living her life under a shroud of guilt but found it difficult to see a way forward. She did not want to trap Anthony in a marriage, however he'd been thrilled when she'd told him she was expecting. Her emotions and her thoughts were at cross purposes, even as she tried to do the right and proper thing, knowing whatever she did would bring pain.

Her sisters and brothers filed into the sitting room that afternoon with their spouses. She stood in front of the fireplace, listening to their happy chatter. She was sick with worry and held a hankie to her nose that had a drop of peppermint oil on it. Her appetite was erratic, but mint continued to be soothing for her, calming her stomach. Elspeth was looking at her speculatively, and Lucinda glanced at her, ignoring her husband teasing Payden.

"Are we having lunch?" Albert asked his wife.

"I don't know," Kirsty replied. "You did just eat breakfast, though. Why are we here, Muireall? What is going on?"

Aunt Murdoch reached up from her chair to hold Muireall's hand. She whispered to her in Gaelic, and it felt as though her mother were near, the words calling her back to an innocent time, a time when her family was whole. Tears threatened, but she knew she must manage her nerves.

Everyone was quiet then, looking at her, waiting for her. Her time of reckoning had come.

"I . . . I . . ." she said on a whisper, then stopped to clear her throat. "I wanted to make everyone aware of some changes, temporary changes, to the Locust Street household for the next few months. I'll need some help during this time."

"Of course you'll have our help, Muireall. But what changes are you talking about?" James asked.

She glanced around the room. She loved everyone there—they were more than mere siblings. Time and change and even distance had not stopped her feelings, only expanded them to Alexander, Lucinda, and Albert.

"I'll be relocating until Christmas. Baltimore most likely. I have an agent looking for an apartment for me . . ."

"Whatever for?" Kirsty asked.

Elspeth shook her head. "What is this about, Muireall?"

She took a deep breath, and Aunt Murdoch squeezed her hand. "I'll be moving away until I've borne a child and seen it settled with a family."

"A child?" someone whispered. She didn't know who had spoken because her eyes were filled with tears. "Mrs. McClintok may need help," she said and nodded to the woman standing in the corner of the room, her hands covering her mouth. Muireall had insisted she be present. She was a member of the family. "And Payden has just turned seventeen. Someone will have to supervise him about his schooling and other issues."

James stood slowly. "Why, for the love of all that's holy, would you be considering moving? Or giving up your child? What are you thinking, Muireall?"

She glanced at her hands, now folded at her waist. "I'm no example for a young man, for my brother, for the Earl of Taviston," she said and turned when Payden jumped to his feet.

"Not an example?" he said hoarsely. "Not an example? You have been everything to this family at the sacrifice of your own life. You are the beating heart of us! You can't go anywhere, sister. I can't allow it."

Kirsty was crying softly on her husband's shoulder. Elspeth stood and walked to Muireall, smiling placidly, as if her sister was not some shameful creature, unworthy of the MacTavish name. She took Muireall's cold, sweating hands in hers.

"How very happy I am for you, Muireall. But you must not leave Locust Street. We must all be nearby during your confinement. You see, we cannot live without you close by, and you must know that any of our troubles are all of our troubles. I love you, sister. You must stay right here."

Elspeth handed her a handkerchief. She dabbed at her face, her determination to not shed a tear gone by the wayside. She looked up when James spoke.

"I think it's downright foolish to leave your home—you must know that, Muireall—but you can commiserate with your sisters and brother all day on that subject. What I want to know right now is who the bastard is who got you in a family way? Who is it, Muireall?"

"Whoever he is, why won't he marry you?" Alexander asked.

"You must not be unkind. Either of you," she said. "He has offered to marry me."

"Then what in the hell are you thinking, woman!" James shouted. "Marry the man."

"He didn't force you, did he?" Albert asked haltingly.

She shook her head, feeling her face redden. "No. I was a willing participant."

"Then what's the problem, Muireall?" James asked again.

"It's Mr. Marcus, isn't it?" Kirsty said.

She nodded.

"Why, Muireall? Why won't you marry him?" Elspeth asked.

And then her anger at her situation got the best of her. "Why? Because I accepted the mantle handed to me as Father and Mother lay dying in their berths as the eldest daughter of an earl. I told them I would raise the family, guard you all, and see everyone settled. It was my life's work," she said shrilly. "I can hardly walk away now!"

"What are you talking about?" James asked. "You've fulfilled your obligation twenty times over."

"You must see to your own happiness, Muireall," Kirsty said with conviction.

"Nothing else is worthy of Mother and Father," Elspeth said.

"Rory and Cullodena would only want you to be happy, dearest," Aunt Murdoch said in her shaky voice. "Their legacy was to see this family safe and content. My God, you've accomplished it all."

"There is still danger, Aunt. You know that."

"There is danger everywhere," James said. "An illness, an accident, a weakness undetected. We must live our best lives in the face of adversity. What are you waiting for?"

"Do you love him, Muireall?" Lucinda asked.

She nodded and whispered. "Yes."

"Does he love you?" Elspeth asked.

"Yes. Yes, he loves her more than life itself," Anthony said from the doorway.

Muireall sagged against the brick fireplace. Her head was spinning, and she was suddenly exhausted. "How long have you been standing there?"

"Long enough to know that you must get off your feet and rest," he said as he approached her and pulled her to his side. "Would you like to go up to your room, or can I convince you to sit down on this sofa so I don't embarrass myself trying to carry you up the steps while juggling a cane?"

The room was silent while Elspeth and Kirsty quickly stood and Muireall sat down. Mrs. McClintok cleared her throat.

"I've tried a recipe from Mrs. Wagner, the neighbor who came from Germany a few years ago, and made pork and sauerkraut with dumplings for lunch. There are fresh cinnamon buns on the counter if anyone wants one until I finish the dumplings, and we'll be having chocolate custard for dessert." Payden jumped from his chair, followed by Alexander and Albert. "The table needs set, gentlemen."

"I know where the silverware is," Albert said.

"Everyone knows where the silverware is." Payden laughed. Alexander was counting place settings out loud as they went through the dining room door.

James bent down to kiss Muireall's forehead before turning with a hand outstretched to Lucinda. Kirsty helped Aunt Murdoch from her chair, and Elspeth took the plaid from the back of the sofa and laid it over Muireall's legs. Elspeth kissed Anthony's cheek. Then they were finally alone.

He scooted her over on the sofa until he had enough room to sit by her hip. "Muireall, love. You must rest. You've exhausted yourself with worry."

"Anthony," she whispered. "I don't know what to do."

"I know you don't, darling. But let your mind settle. This meeting was emotional. Would you like some tea?"

She shook her head. "I would like to close my eyes for just a few moments. I'm all wrung out."

CHAPTER 10

Muireall was napping soundly before Anthony stood up from her side. She was drained, and rightfully so. Her family had rallied around her, much as he suspected they would, and he was tempted to try and convince her that marriage was the only *right* course, but he knew she needed to arrive at her decision on her own. She was a prickly one, the love of his life, he thought and smiled down at her. Certain about a societal position that no longer seemed to matter to anyone in the family but her. She was proud, and that was not a slight. He kissed her softly and pulled the plaid wool over her shoulders.

He walked into the dining room, and James pointed to Muireall's chair at the head of the table. "Best sit down since you'll soon be part of this family."

There was very little conversation, especially from the men at the table, other than appreciative sighs, and he joined them quickly, digging into his plate with gusto, only wishing Ann were here. She already loved Muireall and the rest of the family. She would be thrilled to know she had aunts and uncles beyond his sister and her husband, who they rarely saw.

"You'd best plan a wedding sooner rather than later," James

said. "Muireall would have an ungodly fit if she had to walk down the aisle with a belly like my wife's."

"Dear Lord, James. You are insulting to your sister and to your wife," Elspeth said, glancing at Lucinda.

"I didn't mean it to be insulting . . ."

"However, it was," Lucinda said. "But he is correct. I think sooner rather than later would be best."

Anthony laid down his fork and knife. "I have no intention of haranguing Muireall to marry me. She must come to this decision on her own, and she's well aware of my opinion and feelings and yours now too. I respect her too much to do anything else."

"He's right," the old aunt said. "Our Muireall must think this through in her own way. She's confused right now and feeling fragile as well. We must remember to be gentle."

The plates were cleared, dessert and coffee served, and still Muireall slept. He sat down beside her, prepared to stay until she was awake, although he'd have to get word to Mrs. Smithy and Ann.

"I'll see that she eats and gets changed for bed this evening. She's exhausted, and I think she'll not want an audience," Mrs. McClintok said quietly.

"You may be right."

"I'll tell her you waited but must be home to your daughter."

He stood, leaning heavily on his cane; the day had been fraught for him too. "I imagine you're right, Mrs. McClintok." He glanced at Muireall, sleeping soundly. "I'd just like to be under the same roof as she."

"I think you will be soon, Mr. Marcus. Although perhaps not as soon as you'd like."

MUIREALL DIDN'T RECALL WAKING UP IN THE SITTING ROOM OR someone—it must have been Mrs. McClintok—helping her to her room or out of her clothing and into a nightgown and her bed. She sat up slowly and looked at her watch, usually pinned to her shirt but now laying on the small table near her bed. At least she'd not slept the day away. It was eight o'clock in the morning, the sun shining brightly, although there was still ice sparkling through in the corners of her window. She found warm water in the pitcher on her dresser, stripped, and washed herself from head to toe. She held the warmed rag over her eyes for several minutes, hoping to clear the dry, scratchy redness she'd woken with.

"Good morning," she said to the housekeeper as she walked into the kitchen. "Where is Aunt Murdoch?"

"Elspeth sent her carriage to take her to Kirsty's store. Payden went with her to help her in and out of the carriage. You know Murdoch's been wanting to visit for weeks, and finally the weather seems to have cooperated."

Muireall dropped down on one of the stools surrounding the wooden table where Mrs. McClintok was kneading bread dough. "I've fallen behind with the bread, haven't I?"

"I've the time now with only the five of us here, and half the time Murdoch is staying with one of your sisters or your brother. Would you like tea?"

"I think so. And maybe a piece of bread with butter."

"Here you are," she said a few moments later. "Eat it all. I've put some of the stewed apples we jarred last fall on your plate. You need your strength."

Muireall ate dutifully, her stomach was not revolting.

"Tell me," she said finally and looked up at the housekeeper. "What do you think of my . . . predicament?"

"There really is no predicament. You lay with the man you love. It's true you are not married, but that makes it no less precious. Life is uncertain, and no one should understand that more than you. Robbie was born seven months after I was married, and my husband died trying to stop a dispute between two drunks when our son was not yet one year old. I would do it all again, including the pain, to have him here to see how well our son has turned out. But that cannot be."

"Are you saying that it doesn't matter that I'm unmarried and expecting a child?"

"I'm saying that life, every day of it, is a gift. We never know when it will be our last. Should you have gotten a ring on your finger before you took him to your bed? Maybe, but it doesn't matter now, does it? You are expecting a child from that union, you do love him, and he loves you. What could possibly hold you back?"

"I'm just so ashamed," Muireall said, red-faced, as she looked out the window near the door.

"You're welcome to be ashamed. Welcome to dwell on 'coulds' and 'shoulds.' I'm happy for you to finally have some joy for yourself," she said and stopped her kneading to look her in the eye with a defiant gleam. "Mr. Bamblebit and I have spent some evenings at an inn across town."

"And you have found joy?"

"Not since my dear Kent was alive have I felt this way." She smiled, taking up the kneading again. "Joy and love and anticipation. And pleasure. Physical pleasure as a woman. It's part of love, you know. Part of the bonds of commitment, whether said in a church or said privately."

"I'm so very happy for you."

"Be happy for yourself then too," she replied.

ANTHONY DRESSED CAREFULLY FOR HIS MEETING WITH Muireall. Ann had begged to be included, but when he told her the outing was just for he and Miss Thompson, she had stopped pestering him, a speculative gleam in her eye. He was hoping for the same thing that he felt Ann was wishing for—that they would become a family.

It had been a week since Muireall's emotional family confession, and his work had taken him to New York City and back on Vermeal business during that time. It felt like a lifetime ago since he'd left her sleeping on the sofa, although he'd sent several notes about his upcoming trip out of town and Ann's new school. Muireall had replied politely but impersonally.

But in her last reply, she'd asked if he would stop and see her one afternoon at his convenience. As he rode to Locust Street in his carriage, he thought this meeting would either be the beginning of his future or the end of his dreams. He was startlingly emotional about seeing her. He never felt he'd let feelings get in the way of sound judgment in the past or self-pity overcome his good sense. But that was exactly how he felt. Reluctant yet anxious. Hopeful and terrified at the same time. A soaring heart? He could not let himself dream.

Reynolds stopped the carriage and jumped down to open his door and hand him his cane. "Shall I wait, sir?"

"It is a raw day. Find yourself a tavern or stables and return in an hour."

Anthony started up the steps to knock on the door and panicked. What if she told him within the next five minutes to leave and never come back? He'd be standing on her stoop in the wind with nothing to do but wait in misery. Good Lord! He mustn't think this way. He'd never been a defeatist and didn't intend to begin now.

Muireall opened the door herself. "Please come in. You will catch a chill."

He leaned down and kissed her cheek before she could move away or stop him. She took his coat and hat, red-faced and flustered. She turned without a word, leading him down the hallway to the sitting room. A fire was burning, and several lamps had been lit even though it was midday, although it was blustery and cloudy outside. A tea tray was on the cart by the sofa she'd fallen asleep on.

"Is that some of Mrs. McClintok's cake I see?" he asked in some attempt to cut through the tension he felt.

"It is my chocolate rum cake," she said and blushed. "Anthony."

He smiled fully, glad to hear his name on her lips. "Then I'm sure it will be delicious."

Suddenly, her eyes filled with tears, and he wanted to do nothing more than gather her in his arms.

"What is it, love? Tell me. Would you rather I leave quickly and not subject us to an uncomfortable parting? Please tell me."

She looked up at him, her lip trembling, her eyes blinking with tears clinging to her lashes. He thought she looked radiant.

"I don't deserve a second chance, Anthony, I realize that, but if you would ask me your question again, I'd like the opportunity to answer in a different way."

He propped his cane against the sofa and gingerly bent down on one knee even as she protested. He shook his head as he looked up at her, her hands held tightly against her bosom.

"Muireall Thompson, will you do me the great honor of becoming my wife? I sincerely hope that is the question you wanted me to repeat, dear."

She laughed, as he'd intended, and nodded. "Yes, Anthony. I will marry you."

He pulled himself up and took her hands in his. He kissed her knuckles and looked at her with all the love he felt for her in his eyes. "I will do everything in my power to make you happy. I promise you, on my honor."

"Your honor is why I love you so. Won't you kiss me? I've missed you so much."

He needed no more invitation. He held her face in his hands and kissed her lips softly, staying there, letting each of them get comfortable again in an intimate embrace. Feeling exalted and triumphant and humbled all at the same time. But all of these feelings quickly gave way to passion. He turned his head and deepened the kiss, feeling her pressed against his chest and hearing her soft sounds of acquiescence. He wanted her more than any woman he'd ever known. And she would finally be his.

Being in Anthony's arms felt as though she'd come home, even though she stood in her very own house. She loved him so very much. But she was terrified of change and sharing responsibilities and decision making. She had admitted as much to herself as she let her mind clear over the last week, to look at what she was afraid of, whether it was a love solely hers, which was a great burden on its own, or a loss of independence. But none of those concerns could overshadow the fact that she wanted to spend the rest of her life with him, with Ann, and with this new precious life she carried.

She could hardly believe her good fortune in finding Anthony Marcus, tamping down the niggling feeling that something was bound to go wrong. That she was not deserving of love and that the fates would somehow pull the rug out from under her feet. She would not make herself crazed with doubt. She would not!

He softened his kiss and smiled. "I have dreamt about this. About kissing you."

Suddenly, she felt lighthearted. Girlish and free. "Have you dreamt about my chocolate cake? It is quite delicious."

He laughed. "I didn't know about it until a few moments ago, but I am prepared to make a judgment if you will only cut me a very large piece."

* * *

"We've set the date for April fifteenth. That gives me three weeks to make some plans and yet soon enough, given my condition," Muireall said to her siblings.

"Hopefully, we'll have pleasant weather," Elspeth said with a smile. "How very exciting!"

"It mostly rains in April," Payden said.

"You have not stopped being annoying," Kirsty said and poked him with an elbow.

"We're going to forgo any attendants and have Ann with us at the altar. She will be beside herself with excitement," Muireall said. "I am planning on having James and Payden escort me down the aisle. The ceremony will be at eleven, and we'll have lunch at Alexander and Elspeth's afterward."

"Are you fools going to live under the same roof or no?" James asked.

Muireall felt herself blush. She was feeling particularly sensitive about her siblings knowing she would be living with a man and sleeping in his bed. She knew she was being ridiculous as they all knew what had happened to get her expecting a child, but still it was embarrassing having always thought of herself as the parent in the family.

"I will be living on Spruce Street, of course. If everyone's in agreement about what I mentioned before, then we'll have Mrs. McClintok, Robbie, and Payden continue to live at Locust Street. The house is long paid for, belonging to all of us, as MacTavish monies purchased it originally and kept it in good order all these years. We still continue to funnel the canning business profits into the trusts established to guard the family money."

"You could not talk Payden into coming to live with you?" Kirsty glanced at her brother.

"I'll be eighteen in three months. My schooling will be completed soon, and I've been applying to colleges to continue my education and may not even be living in Philadelphia come September when classes commence. I work several days at James's, some evenings at Kirsty's, and Robbie and I have kept the canning business running. I'm not a child anymore," he said with some vehemence.

"You're not," James said. "You've been raised right and have a man's sense. I see nothing wrong with the arrangement."

"It's not like Mrs. McClintok would let things get out of hand," Elspeth said.

"And Murdoch will move from house to house depending on her whims," Kirsty said. "She's going to Elspeth's for the summer because her gardens are particularly nice and she likes to see MacAvoy and his family too."

Elspeth laughed. "MacAvoy will dote on her, as he's always done. She says he always felt like one of our own, having lived with us after his mother died, even though she constantly questioned his antecedents. James? Do you keep in touch with him?"

"We head to the Water Street Tavern every now and again, but Eleanor keeps him on a tight leash," he said.

"As if your wife doesn't," Kirsty said.

Muireall glanced around the table, and it struck her how much she would miss this, the banter, the Thompson family before husbands and wives had appeared. But she would not begrudge any of them their happiness for all the riches in the world. Locust Street would no longer be the center of the family, and that did sadden her, but her new life would begin in just three weeks.

"Now," Kirsty said. "Let us get to the heart of the matter. What are you wearing for your wedding, Muireall?"

CHAPTER 11

"I am so glad that you have joined us for dinner, Miss Thompson," Ann said as she spread her napkin on her lap. "Papa and I eat at the little table near the kitchen when he is home, but when he is not home, I eat in the kitchen with Mrs. Brewer, the cook, while she bakes bread or makes soup for the next day. This is my first time eating in the dining room, is it not, Papa?"

"I am very glad to join you," Muireall said and glanced at Anthony. Sarah, the maid, and Mrs. Smithy were carrying in platters and helped to serve each of them.

"Thank you, Sarah," Ann said with a smile to the shy maid, who curtsied before hurrying back to the kitchen.

Mrs. Smithy sighed and glanced at Anthony. "She's only been in America for a few months, sir, and worked in some lord's country home in England. I've told her we don't curtsy here, but I think she forgets."

"Don't worry, Mrs. Smithy. She'll get accustomed to our ways, and there's no harm until she does," Anthony said.

"Thank you, Mr. Marcus. I'll tell her you said that. It might make her less anxious." She glanced at the platters. "I'll be back to check on you in a bit, sir."

Anthony waited until the door closed behind the housekeeper. "Would you like to say grace, Ann?"

She closed her eyes and folded her hands in front of her. "Thank you for our meal and for our home and my new school. Thank you, dear Lord, for my Papa and for Miss Thompson too. Amen."

"Before we begin, Miss Thompson and I would like to speak to you," he said as Ann picked up her fork and knife. She laid them down carefully and looked at them both.

Her voice shook when she spoke. "What is it, Papa? Has something happened? Do we have to leave here?" she whispered.

Anthony smiled and pushed his chair back. "Come here, daughter. This is not bad news. We've had plenty of bad news in the past, haven't we?" he said as she climbed into his lap. He wrapped his arms about her. "This is very good news. Miss Thompson has agreed to marry me."

Ann covered her mouth with her hands, glanced over her shoulder at Muireall, and then hugged him tight. Muireall could see her shoulders shaking as she pressed her face into her father's shoulder.

"Ann, darling. What is it? Tell me."

"There is nothing wrong, Papa. I am just so . . . happy. I've dreamed of it."

"Of Miss Thompson marrying your old Papa?"

Ann nodded and climbed down from her father's lap. She hurried to Muireall and stopped abruptly just a few feet away. Muireall pushed back her chair and opened her arms. Ann rushed to her, and then they were both crying and hugging each other.

Muireall had had concerns that a young girl who'd gone through as much turmoil as Ann had might resent Muireall for taking away her beloved father, even though that would never occur. But young girls were sometimes adrift, especially when a family had as many disruptions as Ann's had, so adrift that their emotions could be overwhelming. She kissed Ann's hair and rocked back and forth in her chair. Her vision was a blurry, teary mess, but she could see Anthony walking to them. He knelt down in front of her and held the arms of her chair.

"My girls. I love you both so very much," he said.

Muireall leaned back, smiled at Ann, and wiped her face with her napkin. "Come now, dearest. Our dinner is getting cold. And you did say you were starving!"

Ann kissed her cheek and leaned down to kiss her father's. "I *am* hungry, Papa."

Ann had to know everything then, and she and Anthony indulged her curiosity. She jumped from her chair when they told her she was to stand at the altar with them as the minister married them. She was giddy with excitement.

Anthony smiled indulgently at his daughter, and Muireall wondered if she'd be the one to discipline her if necessary, although Ann had an unnatural ability, Muireall thought, to know boundaries and expectations. She doubted the girl needed more than a gentle reminder, much like Elspeth had been as a young girl, and definitely not like Kirsty, who'd needed stern words and treats denied to make any impact on her behavior. The table was quiet as they ate and Mrs. Smithy refilled their plates and glasses.

"What shall I call Mrs. Thompson and Mrs. Pendergast and Mrs. Watson once you are married?"

Muireall smiled. "They would be honored if you called them Aunt Lucinda, Aunt Elspeth, and Aunt Kirsty. And of course, Uncle James, Uncle Alexander, Uncle Albert and Uncle Payden."

"Do you think?" she said, her face a mask of concentration. "They won't mind?"

"Absolutely not. My nieces and nephews will call me Aunt Muireall and your father Uncle Anthony."

"Then I will be a cousin!"

"Yes, you will," Anthony said.

Muireall glanced at Anthony. They had decided to wait until the wedding was over to tell her she would be a sister in some months. It was Muireall who'd insisted. She'd argued that Ann was very bright and when she was a young woman and meeting young men, she would figure out that this new child was conceived before marriage, and that was hardly the example she wanted to set.

Anthony shook his head and smiled at her. He'd told her that she was worrying unnecessarily about a future event that may never happen. But he didn't naysay her.

Muireall looked up from her plate and found Ann staring at her. "What is it, Ann?"

"What shall I call you?"

"You could me Miss Muireall or something to that effect. Is there something you'd prefer to call me?"

"Yes. I'd like to call you Mama, if you don't mind too much."

"Oh, Ann, darling," she said. "I would like it very much. Very much, dear."

APRIL FIFTEENTH WAS FAST APPROACHING, HE THOUGHT AS Reynolds drove him the short distance to the Vermeal mansion. Anthony had an appointment at the tailor's later in the day since his sisters-in-law-to-be had made it quite clear that he should be wearing something new for his wedding, even though most of his clothing had recently been purchased. He understood, though. This was to be a festive celebration, and he had a key role. He admitted to himself that he was looking forward to their wedding above everything else that had occurred in his life other than Ann's birth, and now there was to be another child.

He climbed down from the carriage, retrieved his leather satchel, and went up the walkway feeling lighthearted. Laurent opened the door for him and took his hat and coat.

"Mr. Vermeal and Mr. Critchfeld are waiting for you in Mr. Vermeal's office."

Anthony knew his way to the office and knocked on the closed door.

"Come," Vermeal said.

Anthony said good morning to both gentlemen, but there was no response. They were both in the sitting area, and he dropped his satchel to join them. "Has something happened? I have not been confident about the Fredrickson deal we are looking at."

"Can you tell us about your first wife?" Critchfeld said, glancing down at the papers in his lap. "Virginia Deloitte Marcus. That is correct? Her maiden name?"

"Yes. That is correct. What is this all about? She's been dead since '65. In a carriage accident."

Vermeal looked at him. "We're not sure she did die, Marcus."

"What in the world are you talking about?" Anthony's heart was pounding, and he stood up from his seat.

"We're not certain yet," Critchfeld said. "This company has a robust security wing, as you know, and we get information from a number of sources, scrupulous and not. We have heard from someone who has given us reliable information before that there is a woman from New York, believed to be dead for the last five years, who has surfaced asking questions about you and a daughter who would be eight years old."

Anthony ran a hand through his hair, his breathing shallow. "I watched her be buried. I held Ann and threw dirt on her casket as it was lowered into the ground. How could this be?"

"Please sit down, Anthony, before you fall down," Vermeal said. "We don't have final confirmation of any of this, but we will."

"Did you see Mrs. Marcus's body before it was buried?"

Anthony shook his head. "No. She had moved out to lodgings above a tavern, and even though I was trying to get her to come home to us, I knew she was involved with something I was unaware of. Opium, I thought at the time. Her mother was an eater. But still I wanted her to come home where she would be safe. We hadn't lived as man and wife since shortly after Ann was born, but I was still her husband and was obligated to see to her care."

"A woman named Virginia Marcus has arrived in Philadelphia and has been telling anyone who will listen that her husband has a job with the richest man in town and that she wants to mend fences."

"Good God! How did she find me? How does she know I am employed by Vermeal Industries?" Anthony looked up at both men. "I'm to be married in less than a week!"

"I'm afraid you will have to cancel those plans for the meantime," Vermeal said. "Critchfeld and I are hoping to get her to agree to a divorce, but it won't happen right away. We aren't even sure where she is staying."

He looked up at them, from one man to the other, both looking at him with serious expressions he'd already seen from them during a sticky or complicated business negotiation. "You mean to pay her off. I can hardly allow it. It is not your problem."

"You will not be squeamish now, Marcus. I'm not doing it for you. I'm doing it for Muireall Thompson, whom I admire greatly. She is a rare woman with the fortitude and single-mindedness to settle a family into a home at a young age and proceed to raise them as if there was nothing out of the ordinary about it at all, and all in the midst of considerable danger. She is remarkable."

Anthony stared at him, feeling lost and angry and irrationally jealous.

"Not in that way, Marcus. Good Lord! She's only a few years older than my own daughter. And she would have never considered me either." He chuckled. "I'm not nearly honorable enough for her."

Anthony bent over, his forearms on his knees, and realized he was shaking. *My God. My dearest Muireall, so concerned that something horrible would happen.* And it had. He saw a pair of shoes beside him and looked up. Critchfeld was holding a glass with some kind of alcohol in it—he could smell it. He couldn't recall if he'd ever drank liquor so shortly after breakfast, but he was needing it now. He swallowed in one swift gulp and wiped his mouth with the back of his hand.

"Can you tell us a little more about the carriage accident?" Critchfeld asked.

"A young boy from the tavern where she was living came to tell me. I hurried to where he said it happened, but her body had already been taken to the undertaker. It was an unreal scene. They had to shoot one of the horses, and several people were injured. They told me that she was in a small carriage and drove right in front of a mail coach. A heavy one was laying on its side. People were shouting and crying and horses neighing. I went to the undertaker's building and rapped on the door of his workroom. He came out and closed the door behind him. He told me there was not much left of her to see, that she'd been under the double wheels and been crushed."

Anthony thought back on that harrowing scene and remembered he'd felt an overwhelming sense of peace, even though he'd felt guilty about it, then and still. But it hadn't been as he'd thought, it seemed.

"What brought you to Philadelphia?"

"Virginia had left outstanding bills in my name all over town. I paid off as many as I could with my savings, but my employment at the time was sporadic. I decided to start over and moved here hoping to be gainfully employed and able to rebuild my savings. It did not work out well until, of course, your company offered me work."

Anthony closed his eyes. Ann would be devastated. They would be back with Mrs. Phillips or somewhere similar, relying on the orphanage to help care for Ann. There would be no school with the other girls and Miss Painter.

"Can you give me time to find another place to live, Mr. Vermeal? I will turn over any documents that I've taken home immediately."

"Are you quitting?" Vermeal asked.

"I can't imagine you'll want a person like me associated with the inner workings of your company. The rumors alone..."

Vermeal stood, poured himself a drink, and handed another to Anthony. "Don't be dramatic. Do you think I'm going to shove little Ann out into the rain? Give me some more credit, won't you? We'll get to the bottom of this, and if it is unsolvable, we may think differently, but there's little that Critchfeld and I haven't been able to solve over the years. Am I right, Earnest?"

"We will solve it, Marcus," he said and looked up. "But I don't envy you the conversation with Miss Thompson."

"You may as well know. She's expecting my child."

"Good Lord. This is a muddle," Vermeal said. "You must go and speak to her right away."

ANTHONY SENT FOR REYNOLDS, WHO PICKED HIM UP QUICKLY and took him to Locust Street. He barely noticed the carriages on the street as he went to the door, hat in hand, with a rolling stomach, although he belatedly wondered who was visiting midmorning. He could not fathom how this had happened. Mrs. McClintok opened the door and smiled broadly. "Oh, Mr. Marcus! Please do come in."

He followed the housekeeper down the hallway, and it seemed as if he was in a tunnel with all the happy family sounds coming from the sitting room muted and far away. He stood at the door, seeing his love, Muireall, laughing gaily at something one of her sisters had said. James came out of the dining room to tell his wife she'd best hurry along all their plans as he had to get to the gymnasium. Anthony watched the tableau as if they were actors on a stage and he was in the audience.

"Anthony!" Muireall said and hurried to him. "What brings you here on a . . . Anthony? What is it? You are white as a ghost."

"Here. Sit down, Mr. Marcus," Elspeth said.

"Ann," Muireall said and put her hand to her throat. "Something has happened to Ann! You must tell me, Anthony."

"Ann is fine," he whispered and then cleared his throat. "I need to speak to you, Miss Thompson. Right away." Her sisters stood, gathering periodicals and yarn and whatnot. "No. Please don't leave, but do give us some privacy, if you will."

He did not want her to be alone after he told her. She would need her family around her. Her sisters hurried out of the room. Her brother James stared at him, hands on his hips, but finally turned and went to the dining room.

"I have upsetting news, Miss Thompson."

"Clearly, Anthony. You must tell me right away."

There was no softening this punch of reality. There was no use making promises he did not know if he could keep. "We must cancel our nuptials. Apparently, my first wife is still alive and has found me."

"What?" she whispered. "What are you talking about?"

"Virginia Marcus is alive and is here in Philadelphia."

Muireall stood abruptly, shook her head, and fainted. He barely caught her in time to get her on the sofa. "Can someone bring smelling salts?" he said in a voice loud enough to be carried into the dining room.

Her sisters and sister-in-law rushed into the room, barking orders to anyone who would listen. A cold cloth was laid on her forehead and her sister tapped her cheeks and called her name. She awoke with a start and stared at him.

"Please tell me that you did not say that your wife is alive," she whispered, which widened every eye in the room.

"I have not seen her, but Mr. Vermeal and Mr. Critchfeld tell me that their sources say she is alive and looking for her husband, who works for the richest man in Philadelphia."

"Tell us everything," James said. "All of it."

Kirsty and the aunt were weeping, but Muireall sat, white-faced and dry-eyed, staring straight ahead. It looked as if she was trying to turn in on herself, not willing to face the terrible facts that he had brought to her doorstep. He'd fallen in love with her, asked her to marry him, planned a wedding, and now he must ruin all her dreams and his too. He dreaded telling Ann.

Anthony told them everything, what he remembered of the day of the carriage accident and what Mr. Vermeal and Critchfeld had found out and that they planned to find her and bribe her to agree to a divorce.

"How does she know where you are? Or who you work for?" Alexander asked. "Do you keep in touch with her family?"

"Heavens, no. Her father left the family when Virginia was young, and her mother relied on opium to get through the day. Virginia and her sister took in wash and cleaned rooms at the inn to put food on the table. I have no idea if the mother is dead or alive—or the sister either."

He looked up and saw James and Alexander glance at each other. "What are you thinking?" he asked.

"Don't know what to think right now, but my security men will find out where she is and what brought her to Philadelphia," Alexander said and turned to Mrs. McClintok. "Do you know where Bamblebit is? I need him."

James looked around the room. "You must all be on your guard at all times. Albert, you must not let Kirsty be alone at the shop. I'll double security at our home, and I'm sure Alexander will as well at his. Tell MacAvoy what is going on. We'll have to get men here. Payden? You and Robbie should go nowhere alone and not far. I'm counting on you to keep Locust Street safe for Muireall and Mrs. McClintok."

Heads bobbed, and James turned to Anthony. "You'd best keep little Ann close by. If this is who I think it is, they would not be above taking a young girl for ransom, mainly for my brother, Payden. And tell Mr. Vermeal that he should not approach her or let anyone in his employ approach her. She may not be dangerous, but we don't know that yet."

"You are thinking this has something to do with this fellow Plowman?" Anthony asked.

"I do. He'll count on us being careless. We must not be."

Muireall stood then, steady on her feet, and left the room without a glance back. He watched her go, watched her walk out of his life. The best woman he'd ever met.

CHAPTER 12

Muireall barely made it to her room, struggling to get her legs and feet to cooperate and navigate the stairs. But she got there, glad no one had followed her. She turned the key in the lock, drew her mother's plaid around her shoulders, and settled into the upholstered chair near her window. She should have known. She really should have. She'd thought everything would be fine, but it was not, and she should have known it would not be fine. She supposed she'd best think about a move again, where she could be a widow with an infant. She had no idea how she thought she'd be able to place this child with a family. She knew now that she could not, but she would not bring shame on the MacTavish clan.

Tears came to her eyes and a deep emptiness in the bottom of stomach. She'd lost the man who'd become dearer to her than life itself. She loved him and was certain he loved her, but they would be separated, and she prayed then that his memory would fade over time. That she'd find some semblance of peace, as she was not certain she could ever feel happiness again. She wept until there were no more tears.

. . .

ANTHONY HAD REYNOLDS DRIVE HIM TO THE PARK NEAR Spruce Street and sent the driver home. He had to think. He had to calm his mind if he was to be any good to anyone, including Muireall. The park was nearly deserted, just a few nursemaids pushing perambulators and a pair of older gentlemen feeding the birds from a paper bag sitting between them. It was clear James and Alexander both thought this was the work of this devil from Scotland trying to get his hands on Payden and therefore in control of what seemed like a vast fortune. He took a look around then, feeling foolish but also taking heed of the warning that James had given them all, including Ann. Good Lord! Ann! He must tell her some version of what was going on, enough to make her cautious, but not so much as to frighten her.

He limped home, his injured leg pushed to its limits with the exercises Albert Watson had suggested. He would admit it felt better overall and had gained strength since he'd started. Anthony was concentrating on his gait, as Albert had suggested, when he turned the corner at 33rd and Spruce. There was a carriage in front of his house with a man slouching inside. He hurried up the walk and into the house.

And that's when he heard it. His dead wife's voice. Speaking as if no time had passed, as if there was no meaning to her obvious deceit. His heart was in his throat as he entered the sitting room and saw Ann standing stiffly, her mother's arm around her shoulders.

"Let her go," he said as he entered. Ann raced to his side.

"We were just becoming reacquainted, Anthony. She's grown up to be a lovely young girl," Virginia Marcus said. "I'd be proud to have her at my side."

Ann leaned against him, and he put his hand on her shoulder. "Pull the bell, Ann."

She hurried to the fireplace, pulled the cord, and ran back. Mrs. Smithy was there quickly.

"Yes, sir. What can I do for you?"

"Find Reynolds and have him guard the door. There's a man outside in a carriage who I do not want in my house. Tell him to load his pistol and station himself in the foyer."

"Right away, sir."

"Don't let anyone in through any door—in fact, make sure they are all locked, and keep the rest of the servants in the house."

Mrs. Smithy hurried from the room. Ann looked up at him. He dearly would like to not have her witness the coming conversation, but he was terrified to let her out of his sight. He knelt in front of her. "Why don't you sit at the low table with one of your books. I need to talk to this woman."

"She said she was my mother," Ann whispered. "Papa?"

"I will explain everything to you later. You must obey Papa in this."

Ann nodded and walked slowly to the low table and chair near the fireplace, glancing over her shoulder at Virginia as she went. He walked to his wife and stood directly in front of her. She was still youthfully pretty, although her eyes were red-rimmed, and her hands shook in her lace gloves. She saw where he looked and held one hand over the other in her lap. She looked up and smiled.

"You're looking well, Anthony," she said.

"Why are you here?"

"Is that any way to greet your wife you've not seen in five years? Surely not."

"You ceased being my wife when you faked your own death, injuring many others in the process. Was I such a very terrible husband, Virginia? That you would leave me to think you'd died tragically and painfully and to leave your own flesh and blood?"

She flitted her hand. "Your job at the War Office kept you away so much. I was young and wanted to enjoy life a bit. You were always so serious."

"Of course I was serious. I'd fought in a war and spent the

next several years tracking down the families of dead or wounded soldiers."

"Well, I wanted to see friends and go out to parties."

"Did the man in the carriage help you stage your death?"

"Heavens, no," she said. "That there's Randolph Patterson. Met him in Baltimore not long ago. The one that planned everything five years ago was Jimmy Weymouth. You remember the Weymouths, don't you? They farmed out on Hostetter Road."

"He just up and said one day, 'Let's fake an accident in the middle of town'?"

"Oh no," she tittered. "Him and me were already stepping out . . . I mean . . . he said he loved me, and I . . ."

He stared at her, at his wife, and wondered, even considering he was lonely and tired and hungry for female companionship when he met her, and she was pretty and liked to flirt with him, how he did not see the defects in her character. *How did I not see?*

"Why are you here?"

She shrugged. "I miss my little Ann," she said and looked up at him with round, innocent eyes. "I miss you too."

"You always were a terrible liar, Virginia. Why are you here?"

"It doesn't seem quite right that you are living so high on the hog, and me, your lawfully wedded wife, scrounging for lodgings and meals, now does it?"

"How did you know where to find me?" he asked, watching her closely.

"Whatever do you mean?"

"You know exactly what I mean. Someone told you where to find me. Was it your new friend, this Patterson fellow?"

"Randolph? No." She shook her head and glanced around. "This is such a pretty room with all this nice, new furniture."

"Who told you where I was?"

She leaned to the side. "Ann, darling? Come say good-bye to your mama. I'll be back and we'll take a walk in the park or shop for ribbons. What do you say?"

"You will not be taking that child out of my sight. Ever," he said in a low voice.

"You would deny me getting to know my only child? You are being cruel, Anthony. Isn't he, Ann? Your father wants to keep you from me! I carried you for nine months and birthed you and raised you. How cruel!"

"Until five years ago, when you walked away from the both of us," he said. "This interview is over."

He walked to the door of the room and waited for her to stand and follow him. Her hands were shaking hard, he could see, and she was blinking rapidly. She waved to Ann and went out the door. He followed her down the stairs and Reynolds opened the door, pistol in hand. She hurried to the carriage once out of the house, and the man yelled something at her.

Anthony gathered the servants together and told them the truth, that the woman was his wife and that he'd believed her dead for the last five years. They were to guard against her entering the house and to let him know right away if they saw her. He locked the front door and turned to see Ann sitting on the steps.

"She's my mother?"

Anthony sat down on the marble beside her. "Yes. She's your mother. My wife. Did you hear what I told them?"

Ann nodded. "She made you think she was dead so she wouldn't have to live with us."

"It wasn't you, dear. Never you. You were the most darling, well-behaved child ever to be. It was me. I was not what she expected when we courted, and she was not what I expected either."

Ann leaned against his arm. "What will happen to Miss Thompson?"

"There'll be no wedding, if that's what you're asking. Not for now anyway."

"Oh, Papa. We love her so much, and she loves us. It's not fair."

"No. It's not fair."

She started to cry, and Anthony pulled her into his lap. "I wanted Miss Thompson to be my mama so much."

"I know, darling. I wanted her to be too."

"Your father is doing what?" Muireall asked Lucinda.

"Mr. Marcus mentioned it the other day when he told us about Mrs. Marcus, but I imagine you heard little of that conversation after he told you he was still married. Papa *was* going to find Anthony's wife and convince her to get a divorce," she said. "He's not now."

Muireall stared at her sister-in-law sitting on her bed while she sat in the chair by the window in her room. She'd not been downstairs for two days. Mrs. McClintok had carried her food and wash water and left it outside the door as she instructed. She really did not want to see anyone and the pity on their faces. But Lucinda was difficult to fool or outlast. She'd sat down in the hallway outside her room until Muireall had helped her off the floor and let her in, and there was not a trace of sympathy in her face. Just her typical brisk, businesslike manner, even though she was due to have her child any day.

"How did you escape James?"

"He is downstairs treating himself to a berry dessert that Mrs. McClintok is famous for."

"The blueberry buckle. She probably made ice cream for on top."

"It looked delicious, but I don't feel as if I could squeeze one more thing into my stomach. There is just no room. I wanted to come talk to you anyway."

"How would you convince someone to get a divorce? It is such a shameful thing."

Lucinda laughed. "Money, Muireall. Money. According to my father and Mr. Critchfeld, Virginia Marcus is unscrupulous and in need of funds. Shame would not be an issue."

"But he's not trying to locate her now?"

"James told him not to. That it may be too dangerous. He and Alexander want to know more about how she got to Philadelphia. James is convinced that Plowman is behind this."

"But what good would bringing Anthony's wife back do? How could that benefit Plowman?"

"I don't know. If I were to guess, I would say he's causing chaos in this family. Perhaps watching for an error on our part. Alexander agrees, although he and James are both rather suspicious men."

"With good reason."

"I spoke to Mr. Marcus today," Lucinda said after a few moments of quiet.

Muireall turned her head sharply. She was so desperate for news of him. She missed him and his daughter, who had been planning to call her Mama. She furiously fought the tears that came to her eyes. "How . . . how is he? How is Ann?"

"His wife came to see him."

"Good Lord."

"Walked in, told the housekeeper some rigmarole, and found Ann in the sitting room. When Mr. Marcus got home, she had her arm around Ann's shoulder, although Ann was visibly upset."

"That poor child! She must be so confused," Muireall said.

"She is. Mr. Marcus said she has been quiet and withdrawn. She overheard his explanation of Virginia to his staff, so she knows her own mother walked away from her when she was quite young. She is very worried about you," Lucinda said. "I sat with her while James spoke to Papa and Mr. Marcus. She told me she'd been looking forward to calling me Aunt Lucinda. She is such a sweet girl."

Muireall was hiding here in her room as if she were a frightened and shameful child. She was not. She was the eldest daughter of the Earl of Taviston and his countess. Her growing love for Anthony, and for Ann, her first experience with the pleasures of the flesh, a new life inside her, all in a matter of a few months had made her hesitant and unsure of herself. That would never do. She must fight for her family and for the all the loves in her life. "I'm going to get dressed and come downstairs."

"Let me help you. We need you."

LATER IN THE EVENING, ANTHONY, JAMES, ALEXANDER, Critchfeld, and Mr. Vermeal all sat in the Vermeal library. A liquor cart had been wheeled close by, and Anthony partook of the brandy. He was adrift. Floating in another man's body, maybe in a lurid novel where the dead person rose from their casket and proclaimed their return to the living. It was nearly more than his orderly mind could take, let alone his emotional one. Virginia Marcus was as scheming now as she'd always been apparently, and unbeknownst to him.

"Plowman is behind this," James said, his burr deepening. "I will kill him with my bare hands."

"You will do nothing of the sort," Vermeal said calmly. "Lucinda is due to give birth to my grandchild any moment, and it would upset her in the extreme if something were to happen to you, although I can hardly credit it."

"I'm going to lead our families' defense," Alexander said. "I've already told James."

"What will I be doing? If you think for one minute I am not going to defend this family, you are wrong," Anthony said.

"You're an emotional wreck, Marcus. Leave it to Alexander. He and MacAvoy will find her and shake the truth out of her, if necessary," James said.

"I can't leave it. My Ann is upset and confused, and I haven't spoken to Muireall for days now. I've got to solve this. This new child will have a father, and it will be me, together with his or her sister and mother."

Critchfeld cleared his throat. "Then you must control all the wild thoughts going through your head and focus completely on whatever task is at hand. This calls for discipline from us all."

"Agreed. I will gladly supply all the money for bribes and whatnot. We've plenty of cash on hand," Vermeal said.

"One of my family's security men, Bamblebit, tracked down the carriage to a livery on the wharf. He's been shoveling out stalls there until they come to rent it again," Alexander said.

"Once we know where their lodgings are, we will move in with plenty of muscle," James said.

"We must all concentrate on keeping our families safe."

"Do you think Muireall will see me?" Anthony asked as he walked out of the Vermeal mansion with James.

"No way to know until you go to Locust Street and ask for her."

Anthony rose early the following morning, did as much work as he could from his office, checked all the doors and windows, and spoke to Reynolds, who had completed all his work in the stable and would be staying in the house with the women. Anthony could see Alexander's man in front of the house, eyes sweeping up and down the street. Anthony drove the gig himself to Locust Street, thinking about what he would say if she would see him. He rapped on the door and noticed two men walking the street, their eyes on him. One nodded, and he nodded back. He saw the curtain at the side window twitch, and soon the door opened.

"It is good to see you, sir," Mrs. McClintok said.

"It is good to know one of the females in this house thinks that," he said and twirled his hat in his hands. "Do you think Miss Thompson will agree to see me?"

"Anthony! Of course I will see you. Can you bring some coffee and cake to the sitting room, Mrs. McClintok?"

The housekeeper hurried away, and Muireall came down the last of the steps. She looked as though she'd like to throw herself in his arms, but he mustn't get ahead of himself. "You're looking well, Muireall. I wasn't sure you'd agree to see me."

He followed her down the hall and through the glass-paned pocket doors to the sitting room. She poured coffee and sliced him a piece of cake after Mrs. McClintok served the cart.

"How is Ann? I'm terribly worried about her," Muireall said.

Anthony blew out a breath. "She is despondent. I think she understands intellectually that her mother is at fault, but that does not mean she doesn't feel bereft. I've told her all of her life that her mother loved her dearly and an accident took her away from us, but now what must she think? Knowing her mother left her, leaving us to think she'd died, that I'd lied to her. Virginia's scheme was diabolical and has made me rethink much of what I've felt was true, but I'm an adult. I understand there are evil people in the world and that I married one. But poor Ann. How can she sort it all out and not conclude that there is something wanting about her?"

"I wish you would bring her here to stay with me during this turmoil. Perhaps I can help her sort it out, although I think she may struggle with this for some time. Girls can be particularly sensitive about this sort of upheaval and tragedy. Elspeth and Kirsty certainly struggled with our family's troubles and the loss of our parents for a long while."

"What about you, Muireall? What are you struggling with?"

She stared at her hands for a few long minutes and finally looked up. "I'm struggling with missing you and Ann. Life is always uncertain, but I was convinced this was my chance for happiness, *my* time. I'm trying to stay positive that somehow it will all work out and that we'll be together as a family, but . . ."

Anthony took her hands in his and squeezed. "I've never in my life been as flummoxed as I was when they told me Virginia was alive. But somehow, some way, we will be a family. I love you. Ann loves you. I will do everything in my power to make sure this child has my name before he or she is born. If you are still willing to marry me, of course. I've wondered if you'd washed your hands of me."

She smiled at him, her lip trembling. "Wash my hands of you? How could I? I sat in my room for two days telling myself I must go somewhere, leave Philadelphia and the family so that no shame would fall on you or on the Thompson name. But that's ridiculous. Everyone I love is here, including you."

Anthony kissed her knuckles. "You must know, Muireall, that if you were to leave, I would find you. Ann and I would find you wherever you are. I don't know how it happened, from that first night I barged into your dining room those short months ago to today, but you and Ann and this new child are my everything. I will always find you, darling. You can't escape."

MUIREALL LOOKED AT HIM AND KNEW THAT HE WAS TELLING her the truth from his heart. She trusted him, and that was a rare feeling for her outside her family members. She had to believe him. She had to. She would run mad otherwise. She kissed his cheek.

"Think about bringing Ann here. It would do us both good, and I could continue her studies with her since you are not sending her to school right now, I don't imagine."

"She is not going to school right now, too risky. She would jump at the chance to stay with you. But I don't want to burden you."

"Burden me? She will never be a burden, ever."

"I must go, dear. I've got to meet with this MacAvoy person and Alexander and hear what they've found out. Maybe we'll know something from Bamblebit too. He tracked down the stables where Virginia rented the gig. Please be careful, and don't leave the house."

Muireall followed him to the door and stepped close to him, looking up into his eyes. She wrapped her arms around his waist and felt him do the same, bringing her close to him from knee to breast. *Ah, how I love him.* "Every time we've dealt with Plowman, events occurred quickly, dangerous ones, surprising us and hoping to wear us down and turn over Payden. Whatever happens, you must know I love you, forever and ever. You must remember that if for some reason we could not tell each other face-to-face. Promise me, Anthony."

He searched her face. "Muireall. You mustn't—"

"Promise me, Anthony. You will remember that I love you and Ann, and I will remember that I have your love in return."

He kissed her deeply then, holding her face in his hands. "I promise," he whispered, and then he was gone.

Muireall was not certain she would ever see him again, but she must be strong. There was no one to be strong for her.

CHAPTER 13

Anthony took himself directly to the Vermeal mansion, where the other men had agreed to meet. He went to Mr. Vermeal's office as directed by Laurent and joined Alexander, James, and Vermeal, all seated on sofas and chairs around a low table. Vermeal explained Critchfeld was out meeting with someone who may have information about Virginia's whereabouts.

A servant opened the door and wheeled in a cart with platters of sandwiches and pots of coffee. He did not think he could eat, but he figured he must force himself in order to face what may come. He was not convinced Plowman was behind this but admitted he did not have experience with this sort of subterfuge. His role in the army had been to charge into enemy lines and kill as many Confederates as possible. There had been no gray area or underlying mission. Not like this situation with decades-old grudges and violence. A tall, thin man came through the door after the servant.

"MacAvoy," James said. "Sit down. We must plan."

"I don't know, James. I'm in me clothes from the mill and might dirty up that fine couch. I'll just stand here and listen."

"Sit down, young man," Vermeal said impatiently. "My neck will be in a permanent crick if I must continue to look up at you."

Anthony moved over on the couch and shook the man's hand when he was seated. Muireall had told him that MacAvoy had been raised as part of their family after his mother had died and that he and James had always been thick.

"You the one who plans on marrying Muireall?" MacAvoy asked.

"I am."

"Probably would have been good to know you were still married before you asked her."

Anthony took a deep breath, and James huffed a laugh.

"Thank you for helping us," Anthony said after he collected himself. "I hear if it is this Plowman fellow who's found my wife and brought her here that he is a dangerous man. I appreciate your willingness to join us."

MacAvoy picked up a sandwich. "Muireall scared the pants off me when I was a youngster and didn't know my ass end from my front. But she was patient with me too, making sure I learned my numbers and reading. Made me feel part of the Thompson family, even though she owed me nothing. Even saw to my poor drunk mother's funeral expenses." He chewed slowly and turned to focus on Anthony. "I would die for her, I would."

Anthony held the other man's eyes and nodded. "I would too."

Alexander cleared his throat. "Bamblebit said that Mrs. Marcus rented the gig again just a few hours ago. She was alone. He couldn't keep up with her to follow. No sign of the man who drove her to your house, Marcus."

"Randolph Patterson is his name according to Virginia," he said.

Vermeal wrote in the notebook on his knee. "I'll see what I can find out about him."

The men ate, shared what little information they'd gathered, and planned fortifications. Anthony hurried home to check in at Spruce Street. All was well, it seemed, although Ann would not come down for her lunch, Mrs. Smithy said. He knocked on her bedroom door and she told him to come in. She was holding a doll in her lap. He thought it might have been the one that she'd carried with her from their rooms on Devlin Street that she'd found at the orphanage. One of the sisters had given it to her to keep.

"Hello, Papa," she said. "Are you done with your work for the day?"

"No, I'm not, but I wanted to see how you were."

"I'm fine, Papa," she said and looked out the window.

But it was clear she was not fine. His happy, smiling, inquisitive girl was instead quiet and tentative. He kissed her hair and chatted to her, begging her silently to come back to him, his darling girl who had turned in on herself.

ANN STOOD BY HER BEDROOM WINDOW, STARING OUT INTO THE large trees in the back gardens, their leaves just opening. Papa had just left her room after checking on her. He'd told her he must go meet with Mr. Thompson but that he would be home in plenty of time for dinner and that they would eat together at the little table near the kitchen.

Mrs. Smithy had asked her to come down for lunch, but she wasn't really hungry, which was strange if she thought overmuch about it as she and her Papa had often been hungry. She'd sometimes claimed she was full when there had been an extra portion of their dinner so that he would get enough to eat. She thought it was likely he'd done the same. She smiled thinking about it and their room at Mrs. Phillips's house. She loved living in their new house with Mrs. Smithy and Mrs. Brewer and Sarah and Reynolds to drive them, but before they'd moved here, she'd had her papa all to herself. She didn't any longer.

The only person she was willing to share him with was Miss

Thompson. She smelled so good! Her eyes were kind and honest too. She loved her, just like her Papa did, but now they would not be able to marry her because her mother had arrived. She looked down at the doll in her hands, fastening and unfastening the buttons on the back of the dress. It was hard to think about that lady, her mother. She didn't like to do it. She had a funny smell, like the back of Mrs. Phillips's closet where she kept old dresses and hats. Her mother had never really looked at her either, even though she had stared into her eyes with her arm around her shoulders. She wondered why.

Just then a small open carriage came down the alley behind their house and stopped beside their gate. She leaned forward and saw that it was her mother waving to her. She could see her through the window, leaning out of her seat. *I wonder what she wants?*

ANTHONY TOOK HIS GIG TO ALEXANDER'S HOUSE TO HEAR directly from the man Bamblebit, who was employed by the Pendergast security staff—and was also sweet on Mrs. McClintok, he'd just learned. The house was a beautiful brick mansion, and he was greeted at the door by a Mrs. MacAvoy. Interesting, as he would never have paired the tall, rangy working man with the very attractive and dignified woman who bid him to follow her. He would have to ask Muireall the story behind that marriage, he thought. He intended to ask her questions and for her to answer for the next fifty or sixty years. He would have her as his wife!

Bamblebit had just begun to tell them that he followed the carriage as far as he could and had been fortunate to see one of the men he worked with on horseback. He'd quickly made his way to him and described the carriage and the driver. The man had gotten a message to him a few minutes ago that the carriage was heading to cross the bridge over the Schuylkill.

"Into these neighborhoods, then?" he asked.

"Yes. Depending on which way she went when she got to this side. Also, where the Vermeals and your home and James's are located too."

"Lucinda is with her Aunt Louisa across town, and our staff have the house locked up tight," James said.

"Father and a few men are on their way here," Alexander said. "They'll make sure Elspeth and Jonathon are safe while I am out. Albert has moved Kirsty to a hotel near the college. I've two men who are part of Pendergast security who will run messages to anyone we need to inform. Or warn."

The door to Alexander's study opened, and they heard excited voices in the hall. Mrs. MacAvoy rushed in.

"Mr. Pendergast, come quickly. You are wanted by Mrs. Pendergast. There is someone here with a message."

The men hurried down the hallway to where Elspeth knelt on the floor holding a young woman in her arms.

"Sarah!" Anthony said when he recognized his young maid. "What is it?"

The girl was panting and crying, and Elspeth was rocking her back and forth, attempting to calm her down. He dropped to his knees.

"Sarah," he said softly, terror filling his throat. "You have come all this way to tell me something of great importance. On foot, I think. Take a breath, please, and tell me what has happened."

The girl nodded and took in great gulps of breath. "Mr. Reynolds . . . got coshed."

"Is he all right?"

"Mrs. Smithy sent Cook for a doctor," she said finally in a thick Cockney accent and looked up at him. "We can't find Miss Ann!"

"What do you mean? She was in her bedroom not an hour ago!" he said, panic rising. He could hear Alexander in the background shouting orders. He wanted everyone armed and handed

Anthony a pistol even as he knelt, too stricken to understand what had happened. Where was his darling girl?

He was to go to his home with Bamblebit and discover what he could if Reynolds had woken. Elspeth would take care of Sarah. He climbed in his gig, and Bamblebit took hold of the reins as Anthony was in no shape to navigate the busy Philadelphia streets. Alexander, MacAvoy, and James would go to Locust Street to guard the homestead.

Anthony jumped down from the gig and pounded on the locked door. "Mrs. Smithy?"

"Mr. Marcus! I can't find her anywhere," the housekeeper said through her tears after letting him inside. "And the back door from the pantry was unlocked."

"Come quick," Mrs. Brewer shouted from the kitchen doorway. "Mr. Reynolds is awake."

Anthony hurried along, his limp plaguing him, the gun heavy in his jacket pocket, until they found Reynolds stretched out on a bench in the mud room, the doctor stitching his head. He wanted nothing more than to pick the man up by the shoulders and shake him until he told Anthony anything he could remember.

"I'm sorry, Mr. Marcus." He winced as the doctor pulled a thread through his scalp. "I ran out to the stable 'cause I thought I saw someone a-lurking there, and then I seen that little one-horse gig that was here before come down the alley. I ran out of the stable to tell them to move along. They must have had a man hiding in the bush there. There was a commotion out front with a horse, and those fellows you hired couldn't get by. It all happened very fast."

"I found him at the back entrance to the stable, on the alley side, blood all over him," Mrs. Brewer said.

Anthony turned to Mrs. Smithy. "You have searched the house thoroughly?"

"Yes. I sent Sarah to Mr. Pendergast's, and Mrs. Brewer and I opened every closet door, looked under every bed, in the attic and the cellars too. She's not here." Mrs. Smithy began to sob. "I should have never let her out of my sight!"

"We will get her back, Mrs. Smithy. Please keep yourselves safe. I don't know when I'll return."

"Bring that girl home, Mr. Marcus. We're all very partial to her," Mrs. Brewer said.

"I will," Anthony said. "I most definitely will bring her home."

"This is Plowman, for certain," Bamblebit said. "This was well organized with a diversion on the front street. All they needed for it to work was for your daughter to hurry to her mother."

"This will be a battle, won't it? There'll be no negotiating?"

Bamblebit shook his head. "No police either. Last time Plowman had gotten to one of the officers."

"Give me five minutes," he said and hurried up the steps, pulling old clothes out of a trunk and finding his Spencer repeating rifle on a high shelf.

"What do you want to ask me?" Virginia Marcus said as she drove the small gig. "I can tell you are bubbling over with questions. Just like I was as a young girl."

Ann was tight against her mother's side on the small seat and glanced up. "Are you saying I'm like you?"

"Of course you are! You're my very own daughter."

Ann shook her head. "Then why did you leave me?"

Her mother flashed her a smile. "Let's talk about something else, dear, not this dreadful stuff your father dwells on. Let's plan our first shopping trip! Your mother will be coming into buckets of money very soon. We can shop for hours!"

"I go shopping with Miss Thompson and her sisters when I need something. Or Papa takes me."

"Well, now your mother is home, and I will take you," Virginia said with an edge to her voice. "And that's enough talk about those snooty Scottish trying to turn you against me."

"They've never said anything against—"

"I won't have it, girl. I won't! You'll learn to mind me!"

Ann shrank back in her seat, trembling. Why, oh why, had she ever agreed to go for a ride with this woman? She waited a while until her mother began to hum a tune to ask her where they were going.

"Why, to Locust Street, girl! To see your precious Miss Thompson. Such a saint, she is, toying with a married man. There's a name for women like her, you know!"

Miss Thompson! Her mama would save her from this woman! She needed to be quiet and patient, and she would be saved.

MUIREALL WAS LOOKING OUT THE BACK WINDOW OF THE kitchen toward the alley, staring off into nothing, having just read a message from a man on horseback that Ann was missing. She was sick with worry. She'd not even told anyone yet. It was as if she had to say that terrible news out loud to make it true. Mrs. McClintok was upstairs changing bedsheets and Robbie and Payden were in the canning room, shadow boxing and planning whatever trouble they could get into, she imagined. She'd best tell them all so everyone could be on their guard. That's when she saw it. A one-horse gig pulled up behind the low fence at the back of their property.

"Ann," she breathed and wrenched open the back door. She ran down the stone walkway toward them.

"Help me!" Ann cried, trying to climb out of the gig. "Mama!"

The woman beside pulled her back and screamed at Muireall. "Something here you want, you trollop? Think you can take my daughter, do you? You'll see! You'll see!"

Muireall ran straight at them, screaming Ann's name, barely noticing a closed carriage that had pulled up right behind the gig. She held out her arms, her skirts swirling around her ankles, running as fast as her feet would take her as Ann squirmed and pulled to be released. But suddenly she was going nowhere, and Ann's eyes grew wide. The woman in the gig screamed at the same time Muireall's world went black.

ANTHONY JUMPED FROM THE GIG JUST AS THEY MADE THE corner of the street, not even waiting for it to stop completely and barely hanging on to his balance. Bamblebit was telling him to go straight to the Thompson home, that he would catch up. He ran as much as his bad leg would allow down Locust Street, having received a note from a rider in Pendergast's employ fifteen minutes earlier as he and Bamblebit left his Spruce Street house and all the chaos there.

The front door was open, and two armed men stood on either side of the stoop. There were other men, hardened-looking ones he did not recognize, in the foyer. He hurried past them.

"Ann! Ann! Where are you?" he shouted as he made his way into the sitting room as fast as he could go.

"Papa!" she screeched and jumped from Mrs. McClintok's lap. "Papa! They took her! You must hurry and get her!"

Anthony dropped to his knees and held out his arms. And then she was there, against him, crying and shivering with fear. His arms closed around her, and he kissed her cheek and her hair, feeling his eyes fill with tears.

"Ann. My dear Ann," he whispered. He held her back from him, looking her up and down. Her dress was torn and filthy on one side. "Are you all right? Does anything hurt?"

"I'll be fine, but you must find Mama! They took her!"

"Ann," Mrs. McClintok said from behind her. "You must let your papa speak to Mr. Thompson and Mr. Pendergast. Will you come with me to the kitchen? I need help there."

Ann hugged him hard, turned away, and took Mrs. McClintok's hand. He heard her ask if all the doors were locked, and it nearly broke his heart. He looked up at James Thompson, who held out his hand. He took it, letting him pull him to his feet.

"What happened?" he asked.

"Alexander and I were only a block away. We heard screaming and raced here. Mrs. McClintok happened to be at a window upstairs and saw everything. Mrs. Marcus pulled up in the alley with Ann, and Muireall went running out the back door. A coach had pulled up behind the gig, and three men climbed off the back and top. One pulled Ann away and threw her into the yard. One grabbed Mrs. Marcus, who Mrs. McClintok seemed to think was surprised that she was being manhandled. The last one put a cloth over Muireall's face and dragged her to the coach."

Anthony swallowed. "They've taken both of them? Why take Virginia?"

"Tying up loose ends, I think," James said. "The men guarding the house out front said a carriage rolled past them the same time they heard Muireall scream. It stopped long enough for a dead body to be rolled out onto the street. Randolph Patterson. Throat slit. Gave Plowman enough time to take the women."

"My God!" Anthony said and stared into the grim faces of Alexander, James, MacAvoy, and Albert.

"Kirsty insisted on coming here when she heard," Watson said. "She said Mrs. McClintok can't d-do it all herself. She's in the kitchen now. Elspeth had to stay with Jonathon and Aunt Murdoch, and Lucinda is nearly ready to d-deliver. I'll fight if I must or tend to the wounded if we are so unfortunate. I've already checked Ann. She's no broken bones, but she'll be bruised and sore."

"I'll fight too. So will Robbie," Payden said. "I'm not hiding here. We've got to rescue Muireall."

"Payden," James barked. "You will not leave this house. This plot is even more sophisticated than when they took Elspeth. They'll know you want in the thick of things, and they'll be waiting for you."

"Payden, please. Muireall has spent her life trying to keep us all safe, especially you. You must listen to James for Muireall's sake. You must," Kirsty said.

"For Muireall's sake," Payden whispered and dropped into a chair. "You must get her back, James."

"Do we have any idea where they've taken them?" Anthony asked.

"The wharf, I think," James said. "We've got several men nosing around down there and should hear soon if they see anything."

CHAPTER 14

Muireall woke slowly, pressed her hand to her head, hoping that would relieve her of the pounding in her skull. It was dark wherever she was and smelled of old fish. Slowly, ever so slowly, images came back to her of seeing Ann reaching for her. She gasped, taking in the rancid air in a gulp. She was sitting on wood, damp wood, and the rocking motion wasn't her imagination—whatever place she was in was drifting, sinking and rising. She was on a boat, and then it all came back to her in a rush. She closed her eyes, praying no harm had come to Ann and that her father had found her. She heard a moan nearby.

Muireall crawled toward the noise, terrified that Ann was here and injured. Light came through wood slats as the boat rocked beneath the afternoon sun, giving her a glimpse of her surroundings. Slimy wood floors and walls and a low ceiling that she was certain she could not stand-up straight under. She heard the noise again, more like a whimper, and inched toward it. She knew as soon as she touched the person that it was not Ann, and her mind raced to think who it may have been, but then she knew. She was captive with Virginia Marcus.

She sat back against the wall, nauseous from the exertion.

There was a taste in her mouth she could not identify, but it must have been whatever drug they'd given her. Anthony must be sick with worry. She scanned the hold, hoping there were no others here, Ann in particular. She could only pray that she would survive this for the sake of her child yet to be born. Plowman. What a curse of a man!

The woman lying next to her moaned again. "Where am I?" she asked.

"In a ship's hold, I think," Muireall said, her throat scratchy and sore.

"I'm going to be sick," the woman said and rolled to her side, retching.

Muireall took breaths through her mouth and inched away. Her pregnancy had disordered her mind and her body, making sounds and smells overwhelming and her tears perpetual over the seemingly smallest of things. But captivity was not a small thing. She hoped she would be as brave as her mother had been during her final hours because, even though she prayed to live and carry this child, there was little doubt that Plowman would kill her. But as long as Payden, the next earl, lived, she would be satisfied she'd done her duty.

How she longed to live, though, to see Anthony and Ann. To see her family. To raise a child and love and be loved. How she longed for that, and because she did, she would fight!

Anthony sat at the kitchen table drinking some water and holding Ann in his lap as they waited for some of Alexander's men to return, hopefully with information. He heard commotion near the front door, put Ann on a stool, and hurried through the dining room. Alexander was speaking to a young red-faced man, tough-looking in a thick sweater over bulging arms with a watch cap on his head.

"Fitzwater Street wharf," the man said, huffing a breath. "I can't say for certain, but I saw a coach fitting the description driving crazy like away from the dock. Saw a ship, a small steamer, old, wooden, not like the iron ones built today. Saw men carrying long rugs over their shoulders and boarding."

Alexander looked at James. "Must be them."

"What is the plan?" Anthony asked. He pulled on his wool coat, thankful he'd thought to change into old clothing, including his army boots, which helped keep his leg stable.

Alexander went to the dining room and spread out a map, giving instructions to certain men, who gathered others and then left the house. Finally, there was only Alexander, James, Albert, Bamblebit, MacAvoy, and himself left in the room, Kirsty Watson hovering at the edge. He could see Alexander had been a smart strategist, spreading men out on nearby streets and sending some to the second floors of warehouses, if they could get in, to scan the scene and place their sniper.

"Where will we be?" Anthony asked.

James shrugged. "'Tis the tricky part here. We're going to get on the boat and rescue Muireall."

"Watson," Alexander said and pointed to a location on a map. "Be prepared to care for men in this storefront."

Anthony glanced around at the men, all knowing that theirs was the deadliest mission, a forlorn hope, as the British referred to these types of frontal assaults. Chances were high that someone around this table would not come back. Bamblebit stepped into the kitchen, and Anthony heard low words from him and soft sobs from Mrs. McClintok. She was promising to care for an aunt of his if he did not come back.

"Lucinda and I spoke early this morning, anticipating this fight," James said quietly. "The doctor said she'll be delivering within the next few days, and you know her father will take good care of her."

"Eleanor will be well taken care of, if necessary, and my girl, Mary, too. Elspeth told me so," MacAvoy said.

Alexander folded the map. "My affairs are in order, and Elspeth will handle the particulars and the needs of any widows."

"Ann," Anthony whispered.

"Will have a home with one of us and be raised as our own daughter unless there's a relative you'd prefer us to contact. Muireall, Elspeth, and I discussed it as soon as we knew Plowman was involved. Muireall said you have a sister. Leaver her direction for me," Kirsty said as she stepped away from the wall. "No matter what happens, Ann will be safe and loved."

"I cannot—" Anthony began and had to stop and compose himself a moment. "I cannot express my gratitude and admiration for each of you in any sufficient manner. But I am grateful and consider myself incredibly fortunate that I will hopefully be part of this family in the future."

James guffawed in the way many men did prior to a battle. "You may not be feeling that way when the bullets are flying!"

MacAvoy and Bamblebit laughed, and Alexander smiled. Kirsty said that men were stupid, but she kissed every one of them and told them each she would see them soon for dinner.

Muireall sat up straight with a sharp intake of breath, seeing Ann reach for her, confused as to where she was. But she remembered soon enough. She must have slept for some amount of time since the light coming through the slats was at a different angle, but she had no idea how long. She felt her leg, looking for the knife she'd been keeping in her skirts ever since they'd realized Plowman was back, but her captors must have discovered it and taken it.

She turned on her hands and knees and began to crawl, running her hands over the slimy walls and floor as she went, hoping to find something she could use as a weapon. She stopped when she touched a coil of rope, found the knotted end, and began to drag it back to where she'd been seated before, where the slats were wider and there was more light. The rope was frayed in places but sturdy enough. She had no idea what she could use it for, but she would figure out something. She heard another moan.

"Help me," Virginia whispered.

"Help you? We are here because of you," Muireall said.

"Please."

"I've nothing to give you. No water, no food, no escape."

"Medicine. Please."

"Where would I get any medicine?"

The woman started to cry, rocking back and forth and reaching out for something, although Muireall had no idea what she'd be reaching for. She was pitiful, but as much as Muireall blamed her and disliked her, her tears and panic were real, and she felt some compassion for her. She crawled toward her.

"You will make yourself sick if you continue to cry and wail," she said and leaned back against the wall beside her.

"I need my medicine." She rolled on her side, facing Muireall, clawing at her sleeve and wailing.

"I don't have any medicine. You must stop this."

Muireall looked up when light poured in, forcing her to cover her eyes. A man leaned down into the hold, although she could barely make out his face in the shadow.

"Our guests are awake, I see!" He laughed.

Virginia pulled herself up on her hands and knees and crawled to him. "I need my medicine. You promised!"

"You'll get it when I say you'll get it!"

"Please! I'm begging you! I'll do anything," she said.

"Anything, huh?"

"Anything," she said and tore at her dress covering her bosom. "Just send it down here, and I'll make it special for you."

"Special? Like giving me the pox? No thank you," he said and slammed the hole shut.

Virginia knelt and pounded on the door above her, screaming

and crying and clawing at the wood. She fell to the floor in a heap, struggling to breathe.

"Calm yourself," Muireall said. "You will make yourself sick."

The woman hurried toward her, and Muireall heard the woman's dress rip and saw her face, wild with panic and fury.

"Give it to me, you bitch! I know you're hiding it," she screamed and launched herself at Muireall.

"I have nothing, Mrs. Marcus. Nothing to give you," she said and held the woman's arms. She was flailing and ranting, but Muireall was stronger and in control of her own wits. "What sort of medicine? What is it that you need so desperately?"

Virginia dropped down, the fight gone out of her suddenly, curling up on Muireall's skirts. "Laudanum. I need it."

Muireall shook her head. An opium addict. She should have known. She'd seen the sisters try and help a woman who had given up her children to the orphanage, and she'd observed no more pitiful person than that woman in her entire life—until now.

"How long have you been an addict?" she asked.

"I'm not an addict," Virginia whimpered.

"Do you always tear the bodice of your dress when speaking to a man, then?" Muireall asked, realizing she was being cruel but unable to stop herself. She would likely not see Anthony or Ann again because of this woman. She hated her.

Virginia drew herself up on her knees. "You have no room to talk! You slept with a married man! My husband!"

"You know as well as I that he believed you were dead from a carriage accident, that he was a widower."

"And what good did that do me? That damned Jimmy," she whispered and started to cry in earnest. "Mum? Mum? Are you there?"

Muireall talked softly to the woman, imagining she was seeing her mother when Muireall knew without a doubt that there was no one else with them. Virginia grew worse by the minute, calling out to others, sweating, and shivering with cold. Muireall drew her up by her side, reaching an arm around her and trying to comfort her. She woke occasionally from her delusions, asking for her medicine. Muireall told her she would have it soon.

ALEXANDER PENDERGAST PROVED TO BE AN EFFECTIVE AND smart commander. He'd told James to go to his wife any number of times since the man received a message from her aunt that all was going smoothly as her niece began her labor. James told them all that Lucinda was adamant that he do everything necessary to save Muireall and that her aunt would be with her during her delivery. It was her contribution to this family danger that her husband would be able to help with a clear conscience. But it was obvious James was worried.

They were holed up in an empty warehouse across the wide wooden wharf from the old steamer, which was bouncing lightly as the water moved to and away from shore. They'd entered the building from a back door at the alley behind the warehouses, opened with a key one of Alexander's men produced. They stayed in a back room, away from the large front windows, although a man was on the second floor watching the ship with a spyglass from behind a dark curtain, just close enough that the lens could peek through.

"We have a man on the roof of the building four down the wharf from here as well. We've got excellent angles, but neither has seen much movement on the ship other than several men hanging about. They're armed, though, so I'm guessing this is the right one," Alexander said.

James walked up to the table where they were all looking at the map of the area. He'd just come in the back entrance with blood on his shirt.

"Caught a couple of Plowman's men in the alley. Sounds like there's two more nests of them. Bamblebit's taken a few men and means to find them. I told him they can't know he's coming, or we risk letting Plowman know we're here. Although it's likely he knows already," James said.

"Where do you have them?" Anthony asked.

James glanced at him. "They're tied up in the back. No use trying to get more from them than I already did. They're low in Plowman's gang and won't know any details."

Anthony wanted to hit someone—or even kill them. He'd always understood that killing during war, while horrifying, was necessary, even though only a few of the men he ultimately killed represented the immorality of the Confederacy. But the rest were, in fact, fighting for the Confederacy, and therefore he could justify their deaths at his, and his men's, hands.

This was different. There was nothing organized, no higher principle at play in this battle. Plowman was an evil and greedy man who deserved to die because he and his henchmen had the temerity to touch Muireall and his daughter in the sick pursuit of a young man. He would relish the chance to kill him.

"We'll go at dusk," Alexander said. "Get some rest if you can."

Anthony knew he could never sleep. He went up the steps to where the man with the spyglass stood and volunteered to take a shift. He leaned against the wall beside the window and moved the curtain enough to see through the glass. Reports were correct. There was little to see except a few men sitting on barrels, one whittling and a few throwing dice against a crate. And then a tall man with a full red beard appeared above deck. Every man there stood. Anthony called down the steps for James and Alexander.

MUIREALL HEARD THE SHUFFLING OF FEET ABOVE HER ON DECK and the loud, deep voice of a man.

"We'll win this, men! We must be diligent! We must be brave! But the disreputable family who's been impersonating the rightful heir of Taviston will be brought down!"

The men shouted and stomped their feet above her. Virginia

stirred awake, twitching now and gnawing at her hand. The hatch opened, and Muireall turned her head until her eyes could adjust to the bright light of the sun.

"Come on, girlies," the man who'd stuck his head in the opening earlier said.

Virginia scrambled to the door, reaching up and letting the man pull her onto the deck. Muireall could hear the men's laughter and crawled to where the man's hand was waving. She dragged the rope with her and pushed it against the wall and into the shadows. She stood in the opening, and a man reached down to grab her under the arms. She ignored him and put her foot on a crossbeam, hoisting herself to a sitting position on the deck, her legs dangling in the hatch. She got to her knees, stood, and smoothed her skirts with as much dignity as she could. She looked around until she spotted a tall man with a full red beard watching her. She met his eyes and raised a brow.

"Mr. Plowman, I presume."

He stared at her, and she did not look away.

"Miss Muireall Thompson. Leader of the clan of imposters who have tried to steal my birthright!"

The crowd of men surrounding him cheered and clapped. Muireall looked at the men, at each man individually, until the deck was silent other than the slap of the waves against the sides of the ship. She turned back to Plowman. "A leader of a great Scottish clan would never be cruel for cruelty's sake," she said and pointed to Virginia.

"Here you are, whore." Plowman tossed a vial in the air near the woman. Virginia scrabbled to where it landed and cried when one of the men kicked it away from her. She finally got it in her hands, pulled the stopper, and put the vial to her lips.

"Not so fast," one of the men said and tried to pull the vial from her mouth. "We's hoping to have some fun with this one later."

Virginia dropped onto her back, convulsing and drooling. Her eyes rolled back in her head, and her hands twitched. It would be a miracle if the woman lived. Muireall tore her eyes away and looked up at Plowman.

"A clan leader would never harass, chase, or threaten death to a woman or kill one unable to defend herself. A clan leader would fight in the open for his clan's honor. And certainly the Earl of Taviston would never attempt to claim the title through murder."

She did not see the blow coming, did not comprehend the pain until her knees hit the deck with a hard jolt. Her mouth filled with blood, and the wood slats of the deck spun before her eyes. She shook her head while Plowman and his men laughed. She straightened, waiting for her head to stop spinning, and stood. She spit blood onto the deck and faced Plowman.

"What a pitiful imposter you are, not fit to kiss the kilt of the true Earl of Taviston," she said. She saw the slap coming this time but could not dodge it. His hand launched her across the deck to land in front of several men, who looked down at her without a word and then back at Plowman.

She took in several long slow breaths, letting the pain ebb and feeling her anger rise. She pulled herself up again and faced him.

"Good God, Muireall, stay down!" James said tightly as he and Anthony and Alexander watched the tableau occurring on the deck of the ship.

"She won't, will she, though?" Alexander asked and winced when she flew onto the deck in front of a line of men.

Anthony watched her pull herself to a sitting position, shake her head, and get on all fours. The tall man who'd hit her was laughing and speechifying, but many of his men were watching Muireall. Stay down, woman! But she would not stay down. She would rise with her dying breath. She stood, staggering, reaching out to steady herself blindly, walking toward Plowman.

"My God! She spit in his face!" James said.

But Anthony heard little of anything else that was said as he was racing down the stairs, through the room they'd been huddled in, picking up his Spencer as he went, hearing the shouts of Alexander behind him. James caught up to him and grabbed his arm, stopping him in his tracks.

"Let me go!" he roared.

James shook his head. "Nay! At least give us five minutes to alert the rest of the men we're storming the boat."

Anthony closed his eyes. "I can't take it, James. I can't watch her being abused. I'll wait for five minutes and not more," he said and looked the boxer in the eye.

He waited four and a half minutes, opened the front door of the building, and charged onto the wharf. Stopping halfway across as he pulled his rifle to his shoulder, he shot a man on the opposite side of the deck away from Muireall. He was terrified the ship would rock or rise and fall and she would be caught in the crossfire, but they had to take the advantage of surprise. He pushed the lever down, expelling the empty shell, cocked the hammer, and fired again.

Anthony heard a war cry come from behind him as James Thompson flew past him running at full speed. He launched himself from the wharf onto ropes hanging over the side of the ship, climbing up and throwing himself onto the deck. It was an incredibly foolish stunt but one that had every man on the boat scurrying for cover or weapons and their men charging at the ship, shouting and firing. Alexander ran to the wharf's edge, firing rapidly from pistols in each hand and giving James cover on a ship full of his enemies while men worked to get a gangplank in place and secure the boat against the dock.

Anthony ran toward the ship, hearing the hiss of bullets as the Plowman gang returned fire. Albert Watson was dragging an injured man away from the fray as Anthony boarded the ship and dropped to his knees, his leg giving out on him. Bamblebit was right behind him and shot a man whose sword was aimed at

Anthony's chest, taking a blade to the shoulder for his trouble. He pulled the knife out of his arm and threw it with unnerving accuracy into the back of the man fighting James.

Anthony climbed to his feet. "Muireall!" he screamed through the smoke and mayhem of the battle. "Muireall!"

He was waylaid immediately by a fist to his chin. He wielded his Spencer like a club and hit the man with the flat side of the stock on the side of his head. The man dropped to his knees, and Anthony pushed past him. He could hear James still shouting his battle cry as he threw men overboard. MacAvoy and Alexander stood back-to-back, punching and kicking their opponents and defending each other's blind side.

He was frantic to find her. "Muireall!"

That was when an explosion rocked the ship, and the air charged as if lightning had struck. He was dropped to his knees again and scrabbled away to the side of the steps leading below deck as Plowman's men were rushing to the gangplank to escape, trampling him as they did. He would not leave without her.

CHAPTER 15

Muireall rarely lost control; in fact, she'd made it part of her life's work to remain calm, stoic even, when faced with difficulties, although this child growing within her had made her a watering pot. Her lip was split open, her chin and cheek radiated pain, and she thought it possible that a rib or two had broken when she landed hard on a metal winch bolted to the deck in front of Plowman's men. Her vision swam before her eyes, men and objects moving in and out of focus, and the words from Plowman's mouth were muted, as if she heard them at the end of a long tunnel. She had forced herself to her feet, knowing full well that whatever punishment he would exact on her would be exacted on her unborn child. She knew all of that. But then she'd rarely lost control.

It did not stop her. The thought of stopping never entered her mind, as her control had disappeared to be replaced with a lifetime of anger and hatred for this man who had caused pain and sorrow and death to those dearest to her. She weaved unsteadily toward him, knowing his men were watching her. Plowman stood, a smirk on his face, his beefy arms crossed over his chest. She got within a foot or two from him, a dangerous distance in reach of his fists, but she did not care. There was plenty of blood in her mouth that would be best not swallowed. She spit it at him instead.

His hand moved quickly, wrapping his fingers in her hair that had tumbled down from its pins, dragging her back toward the hold. She fought him, reaching around wildly, trying to lay her hands on something to use as a weapon. He stopped at the hatch to the hold, picked her up by her neck, and shook her. She clawed at his hands, trying to draw air, feeling herself begin to lose consciousness when he dropped her through the open hold and turned to his men, laughing as he did.

He hadn't closed the hatch and was standing at the very edge. She grabbed wildly for the rope on the floor and stretched her arms out of the hold, looping the rope around his booted feet while he praised his own courage and quick thinking, telling the assembled men that the garbage was now in the hold. She yanked the rope with all her might, dropping on to her knees on the slick floor. And that was when she heard a gunshot and the shouts of men on the deck to arm themselves.

She fully expected Plowman to pitch forward if her maneuver with the rope worked; however, he fell backward as he tried to disentangle his feet, landing awkwardly, his legs catching on one side of the hatch and his head slamming with a dull crunch on the other wooden edge. He fell through in a great heap on top of her. She scrambled out from under his massive body, using the last of her strength, panting and wheezing on all fours as she did, and tied his feet tightly with the rope and then to a post near the hatch. At least she might be able to get away from him if he woke. The shouting on deck grew louder, and she recognized the warrior cry of James Thompson.

Muireall worked to get her feet under her so she could see the mayhem that she could hear happening on the deck just as a man tumbled her way, hitting the hatch and closing it with a thump. She tried to lift it but couldn't move it at all. The man who fell on it was dead or unconscious. She would not be able to escape until someone moved the body, she thought and backed up to lean against a wall and try to get control of her breathing. That's when she heard the explosion and the clamoring of heels above her, even as her ears rang. The ship began to list; she could feel it shifting in the water.

"Muireall!" she heard from above. She scrambled onto her haunches and shouted.

"Anthony? Anthony!"

The explosion had woken Plowman, who managed to untie his feet while Muireall shouted and pounded on the hatch door. He roared and hit her hard in the head with his closed fist. "Bitch," he shouted.

ANTHONY TURNED HIS HEAD FROM SIDE TO SIDE, TRYING TO find the direction of the faint voice he heard calling his name. Where was she? Many of Plowman's men had fled and some of the smoke had cleared as Anthony raced around the deck, searching for Muireall, stopping to kick the gun from the hand of a bleeding man lying on the deck aiming a wobbling pistol at Alexander. He shouted her name again and heard James shouting her name too.

"There!" MacAvoy shouted. "He's got her! There!"

Anthony turned and saw the red-haired man with Muireall draped over his shoulder. The man took one look at the remnants of the battle and took off at a run to the other end of the ship. He stopped and turned back to them at the railing, the ship now listing so much that Anthony had to brace a foot against a deck post as he dropped to his knees and aimed his Spencer.

"Go ahead, shoot me! She'll go overboard with me!" Plowman shouted and then looked up to see James climbing a rope attached to the massive ship stack. He pulled a gun from his side and fired. The ship heaved, its sides groaning and shifting, causing Plowman to lose his grip on Muireall. She dropped to the deck a moment before Anthony fired his rifle, hitting the man in the chest and knocking him backward, over the rail and into the water.

James dropped from the rope and skidded to a stop at Muireall. He picked her up and turned, heading for the wharf. "Go! Go!" he shouted. "She's going to sink!"

Anthony clamored up and used his spent rifle as a cane. He nearly tripped over Virginia's body. She moaned and turned on her side. He put an arm under hers and dragged her toward the gangplank, now leaning precariously. Bamblebit grabbed her other arm, and the two men scrambled to the outstretched hands on the wharf. Bamblebit flung her to them, the men catching her midair and pulling her to safety.

"Go," Anthony shouted to Bamblebit. "Go!"

He wasn't sure he had the strength left to hoist himself onto the ropes Alexander and James and the other men were holding after tossing the men his Spencer. He could barely stand, even holding the railing as the ship heaved, watching Bamblebit launch himself to the netting, grabbing on with one hand, as his other one was covered in blood. Alexander was shouting at him, and he pulled himself to his feet, dragging himself along the rail to where he could get to the fishing nets, but his leg gave way, and he began to roll down the deck as the ship tilted.

James climbed down the nets, reaching his arms through the openings, Alexander and MacAvoy holding the ropes, and held out his hands. "Come along, then, Marcus. Your Ann will be wanting to see you whole and hearty. Come along, man."

Anthony crawled up the deck, grabbing at the railing, pulling himself up, scrambling over the rail bar, and launching himself with his good leg and a prayer as the ship began its descent into the ocean. James had him by one wrist and held tight as the other men pulled them both onto the wharf.

Anthony rolled onto his back, heaving breaths, the fear and

excitement receding, leaving him weak and dazed. "Is she . . . ?" he wheezed when Albert bent over him. "Is she alive?"

"She is," he said briskly. "But she is hurt. We're taking her to the hospital."

"The baby?" he asked, feeling tears gather in his eyes.

Albert shook his head. "We don't know yet. We just d-don't know."

Anthony turned his head and watched as the men carried Bamblebit to the warehouse where Watson was tending the wounded. "Easy," Watson shouted as Bamblebit groaned and slumped. Anthony could not move himself, could barely roll on his side when he thought he might be ill. He could see Alexander helping men to their feet, patting them on the back, shaking their hands, and speaking quietly to them.

James was sitting near Anthony's outstretched legs, his knees drawn up and his head in his hands. His shoulders shook, and Anthony heard a sniffle. "James. James? Are you hurt?"

He shook his head and looked up with suspiciously bright eyes. "I'm just praying he's dead. Thanking the dear Lord your aim was true, on a ship nearly upended. Praying to the Almighty that our family's danger is over and that my sister and her babe will be well," he said and then grinned. "Thank God we got you off that boat before it went down. Muireall would have had words for us if we hadn't."

"Did we lose any men?"

"I don't think so, but we've got some serious injuries," James said and met his eyes. "Your wife is alive, although Albert said she was not in good shape."

"I never wished her dead, even when I thought she had died and that Ann's and my life would be infinitely better without her. But I never wished her any harm," he said as he looked around the wharf and the police officers starting to swarm their way. "But I hate her, my dear girl's mother, for bringing danger to us and to your family."

James stood slowly and put out a hand to him. "Come along. We're just two drunks now when the officers ask us what we're doing here and what we know about the sinking ship behind us."

Anthony got to his feet, wobbling and light-headed. "We won't have to pretend to stagger, will we?"

James laughed, slung an arm around his shoulder, and started singing rather loudly.

MUIREALL WOKE IN A STRANGE ROOM, GROGGY, HEARING muted voices and unable to open her left eye. She could see a thin ribbon of the activity going on around her through her right eye and was just beginning to comprehend the pounding in her head that caused her to moan aloud.

Albert Watson came into view. He picked up her hand. "Muireall. Can you hear me? Squeeze my hand if you can. Excellent! You're at the hospital, and we're going to make you comfortable with some morphine to get you through the worst of the p-pain."

She shook her head, bringing on a welling of nausea. "No," she said through brittle, torn lips. "No. Laudanum. No. Morphine."

Albert tilted his head. "You will be in significant p-pain for several days, even weeks, Muireall."

"No. Laudanum."

Albert stared at her thoughtfully. "Virginia Marcus is in sorry shape. There'll be no opioids for you after seeing her, I imagine. We will get some willow bark tea in you and make you as c-comfortable as possible."

She watched him turn to others in the room, giving instructions for her care. The inside of her mouth was swollen and cut. She ran her tongue over her teeth and was glad that they were all still there, only one a bit loose. She stretched her fingers and found the smallest finger on her right hand wrapped tight against the next one and realized that it was to her benefit to not breathe too deeply and avoid the sharp pain in her sides. It did not feel as though there was a spot on her body that was not in aching or throbbing, but after watching Virginia Marcus groan and beg for her "medicine," Muireall did not want to take a chance that she'd become addicted.

How might those drugs affect the child growing inside of her? If he or she were still growing inside of her. She commanded herself not to cry as she imagined her tears would only add to her misery when they rolled down her cheeks into the cuts on her face. She lifted a hand.

Albert hurried to her side. "Have you changed your m-mind? About the laudanum?"

She shook her head slowly. "The baby?"

Albert held her hand gently between his. "You have not miscarried. B-but you must be realistic. This kind of physical and emotional shock and strain are not good for a child in the womb."

Muireall closed her eyes. Virginia Marcus lived, and Anthony was still married to her. But she must not be greedy. She was alive, and so was this child. If she was never to have Ann as a daughter and Anthony as her husband, she would be forever grateful if the child she carried now lived.

"Alexander? James? The others?" she asked and took a slow breath. "Mr. Marcus?"

"They are all alive and reasonably hearty. Alexander has some b-bruises and a few superficial cuts. MacAvoy has a few scrapes, and Bamblebit has a nasty stab wound that we will watch closely for infection. James's nose is broken, but then I've rarely seen James without a b-broken nose." He smiled. "Mr. Marcus is here. A broken bone, some cuts, and his leg is injured. He shouldn't be on it for several weeks, I don't think."

"Thank God," she whispered and said a silent prayer.

"Ah, here is your sister, c-come to see you," Albert said.

"Muireall?" Elspeth said. "Are you awake? Can you talk?"

She turned her head to see out of the slit of her opened eye. "They're alive."

"Yes," Elspeth said as she smiled and brushed the hair gently from Muireall's face. "They live. Thank the dear Lord."

"Ann? Where is Ann?"

"She's with Mrs. McClintok and Kirsty. She was fine once she heard you'd been recovered and that her father was all right."

"Her mother lives. Mr. Marcus's wife," she said, realizing then she'd best put distance between the two of them. He was no longer Anthony to her. He had healing to do and a spouse in the need of convalescence. "He will have to care for her now. She's not doing well."

"I think it's best right now to think about you, Muireall. About your health and the health of that baby you're carrying. Albert said we can take you home in a few days after some of your injuries have healed. Payden and Robbie will move a bed downstairs for you if you want. I wanted to take you to our house, but we decided you'd be more comfortable in your own home."

"Yes. Home."

"You must rest now," Elspeth said. "I'm going to check on James and Mr. Bamblebit. I'll see how Mr. Marcus is doing as well."

She turned her head away. "I hope he is well, for Ann's sake. I am tired now."

She felt her sister's lips on her forehead and closed her eyes. She was hoping her dreams did not include nightmares.

ANTHONY WHEELED HIMSELF IN THE CHAIR ALBERT WATSON had insisted he use, even going so far as to ask him how he intended to support Ann if he could not walk. His leg was propped up now on a footrest that had been built up so his leg was stretched straight in front of him. It throbbed, robbing him of breath and thought on occasion. He'd nearly taken a dose of opium when he'd first arrived, but then he'd had a glimpse of Virginia, who appeared comatose but was still breathing. It stopped him. The beautiful, cheerful young woman he'd known when he married her was gone, replaced by a woman who appeared to be twice her age of twenty-seven, her face drawn and her skin sallow. It made him sad and angry in equal parts, but it compelled him to battle through this pain in any other way possible.

"I want to see Muireall," he said to Albert.

"She is sleeping."

"I just want to see her." He saw Elspeth leaving a room down the hall. "Mrs. Pendergast. Elspeth. Can I see your sister?"

"Mr. Marcus, how are you feeling?" she replied.

"The doctor here insists I use this chair for now, but I am most concerned about Muireall. I have not seen her since James carried her past me off that damned boat."

"She is sleeping. I'll tell her you've asked about her."

Anthony stared at her and glanced at Watson. Neither were looking directly at him, their eyes skimming away from his. "What? What is it? Please tell me? Is it the babe?"

"Muireall has not miscarried, and I am hopeful she will be fine with rest," Albert said.

Anthony looked at Elspeth.

"Your wife lives, Mr. Marcus. I'm sure she will need all of your attention," she said.

She was not being unkind. In fact, he thought she was trying to let him down gently. Trying to make his pain-addled brain understand that he was still married and that his wife lived. Good God! He turned his chair in the narrow hallway and guided himself back to his room, where he asked an attendant to help him into his bed. He was certain the pain of heartbreak was more devastating than even the pain of his disfigured leg.

. . .

A FULL WEEK LATER, JAMES CARRIED MUIREALL THE SHORT distance from his carriage to 75 Locust Street, through the front door, and into the parlor. "My God, woman! Have you gained a stone or two while taking your rest at the hospital?"

"James! What a thing to say!" Kirsty said as she held the door open. "She's lost weight, if anything!"

James laughed, and Muireall thought she might have smiled at Kirsty's indignation if her lips were healed, but she did not want to make them bleed.

"He cannot resist being an ass," she said instead, making Payden and Kirsty laugh out loud. "Especially now that he is a proud father."

"I'll have you know that little Maeve Thompson is the most beautiful girl child ever born. I have every right to crow," he said, smiling.

"How is Lucinda faring?" she asked.

"If her father and I allowed it, she'd be back at work even today," he said.

"Allowed it?" Kirsty asked with a laugh.

James scowled. "She is the most stubborn woman I've ever met, even more so than my sisters."

"Which means she is doing what she wants to do with her doctor's advice in mind," Muireall said and leaned back slowly onto the cushions behind her head.

She'd been at the hospital more than a week by her count. Many of her bruises had faded to yellow, and the headache that had been her constant companion was beginning to fade too. She'd been given excellent care under Albert's watch, but she was ready to be in her own home. Navigating the stairs might be challenging, but Kirsty was staying for a few nights, and Mrs. McClintok, Payden, and Robbie would be on hand too. Muireall was exhausted now, even though she'd not taken a step without an arm for support and had been carried to and from a carriage. Kirsty must have noticed her fatigue.

"Come along now, everyone, and keep your voices to a low roar. Muireall needs to take a nap," she said and shooed everyone, including herself, from the parlor.

Muireall closed her eyes. It did not take her long to fall asleep in earnest.

CHAPTER 16

Anthony rose slowly from his desk. He was determined to limit his time spent in the wheeled chair that had been sent home with him when he left the hospital. He'd followed Watson's orders to stay off the leg for a full week and to continue the stretching and exercises he'd been doing that had helped his mobility and strength until, of course, he'd jumped on and off a sinking ship. His cuts and bruises had mostly healed, so he'd had a conversation with Mr. Vermeal to ask if he could begin work again at the Vermeal offices, and more importantly, if he was still wanted as an employee. Vermeal had looked at him strangely and told him to get to work as he was busy with his new granddaughter.

He'd had one of the secretaries bring reading material to his home to begin catching up on the multiple projects that he would have to be prepared to direct or make recommendations on. He looked up to see Ann standing in the doorway of his office.

"Ann, dear," he said. "Have you made up your mind about whether or not you will go to school tomorrow?" She shook her head and walked to his desk. He pushed back his chair and waited until she was close to him. "What are your reasons for not going back?"

"I know you want me to go, Papa. I would like to go," she said as she climbed on his lap and leaned back against his chest.

"You're getting too big for your papa to hold!" He laughed.

She turned her head to look at him, her face drawn and serious. "Am I hurting you? I'll get down." She began to move off his lap.

He pulled her back. "Of course not. Now tell me why you don't know if you'll be going to school tomorrow."

She shrugged.

"What is it, Ann?" he said softly.

"I'm afraid to go, and I'm afraid to stay."

"Why are you afraid to stay? This is your very own house."

"Because she's here," Ann whispered.

"Listen to me. She is in a bedroom on the third floor with a full-time nurse to care for her. She is not awake and may never wake up, and even if she did, she would be very weak. She could not hurt you."

"But she stole me away," she said.

"The men who asked her to do that are dead, and she is in no physical shape to plot or plan anything that would harm you."

Ann nodded.

"Do you want to see your friends and go back to school?"

She was silent for a long moment. "Will they know what happened?"

"I've spoken to Miss Painter. She knows what has happened, but she will not allow anyone to gossip about it or speculate. And if they do so outside of Miss Painter's hearing, then you must hold your head up. You were in no way to blame."

She climbed off his lap and went to the door. She stopped and turned to him. "I'll ask Mrs. Smithy if my school dresses need to be pressed."

"I'll tell Mr. Reynolds to be prepared to take you and return home with you from school tomorrow, then."

Anthony climbed to the third floor with the help of his cane after kissing Ann good night. He tapped softly on the door, and it was soon opened by one of the attendants Watson had engaged for him to care for Virginia.

"Good evening, Mr. Marcus," the young woman said.

"How is she?" he asked. It was nearly impossible for him to say "Mrs. Marcus." He hadn't had a wife for five years, and the only wife he would acknowledge now was Muireall Thompson, although he had been "encouraged" not to visit. He inquired after her every day by messenger.

The woman glanced at the bed where Virginia lay, propped up on pillows. "She is not responsive, and I can barely get any water into her. She is breathing better now that we have her more upright."

He nodded and thanked the young woman, then made his way slowly down the stairs. Watson had told him that without nourishment, especially water, Virginia would not last more than a few weeks. Was it cruel to wish a poor soul who was not really alive but not yet dead to pass on to the afterlife? He no longer felt any anger toward her. It felt wrong to hate such a pitiful person who was ruled by opium. Once she had lost the ability to rid herself of the drug, there was nothing to do but feel sorry for her, even knowing she'd put his daughter and Muireall in such danger. But he was concerned that Ann would not feel comfortable, not be the happy girl she'd always been, especially in circumstances that were less than ideal, until Virginia was no longer there. And even then, he was concerned her terror would not lessen for a long time.

The following morning, Ann was dressed for school when she joined him at breakfast. Reynolds would take him to his office and return for Ann. She was subdued but not, he thought, unhappy.

"When are we going to see Miss Thompson?" she asked after Mrs. Smithy served them their meal.

He'd been dreading that question. "We won't be going to see Miss Thompson, Ann. I am a married man, and my wife is in residence. It would not be proper, and Miss Thompson would not allow it."

"My mother, you mean."

"Yes. Your mother is my wife. A person takes vows when they marry another person to honor them through sickness and health. Your mother is very ill."

"But she did not honor you, did she, or me when she ran away from home and made everyone believe she'd died," she replied rather forcefully. "She didn't honor her vows at all."

Anthony laid down his fork. "Who told you that? It is not the type of thing you should hear."

"I'm not a child anymore, Papa. I know what people are talking about when they don't think I'm listening."

He was ready to chastise her for eavesdropping when Mrs. Smithy returned to warm his coffee. But was it her fault that her mother had done those things? No. No, it wasn't.

"Mr. Reynolds has the carriage out front, sir," Mrs. Smithy said. "Whenever you're ready. I'll see Miss Ann in the carriage when he returns."

"Thank you, Mrs. Smithy," he said and looked at Ann. "Give your papa a kiss, please."

Muireall enjoyed a walk outside unassisted as May brought sunny weather. She was three months along, and her stomach was rounded now and her breasts tender. She'd not been bothered by any nausea in the last few weeks, and her injuries were healing. Albert had examined her and said he felt her rib was knitting together, although he still did not want her lifting anything or doing any strenuous work. She harrumphed. Her family was cosseting her to the point that she was ready to tell them to leave off their hovering, even though she knew they did it out of love and caring. Her cheekbone was still tender, and Albert thought it may have been fractured too. But her cuts had healed with the help of Aunt Murdoch's creams and potions and her tender care.

It had almost been decided that Aunt would live with Elspeth and Alexander permanently since they were converting two rooms on their first floor to a bedroom and a sitting room. Aunt could barely make it up the steps here and seemed suddenly frail. Muireall was having a difficult time imagining her daily life without her, but she must consider her aunt's comfort, not her own. Murdoch was sitting on a chair Payden had carried outside for her, enjoying the sun too.

"Don't be wandering too far now, Muireall. You're not long out of a sickbed and a babe to worry about too," Aunt said as she walked down the path toward the alley. Muireall could see herself racing down the stone path that day, her skirts flying, her arms outstretched to Ann, who was calling to her. "Mama," she'd cried.

"I'm fine, Aunt, just enjoying the sunshine."

She stood for a while at the back gate, looking at where Virginia Marcus had stopped the buggy and Plowman's men had pulled up behind her. Muireall had been terrified, terrorized that day and the ones that followed until she awoke to Albert Watson's smile. Remarkably, she'd had no nightmares. Maybe because during her waking hours the littlest thing could focus her mind on an event of her time in captivity. She turned and walked toward Aunt Murdoch.

"What are you going to do about Anthony Marcus?" her aunt asked.

"We've had this discussion already. There's nothing to do. He's a married man," she said and looked down at her folded hands.

"Dear Lord, girl! I give the man credit for taking in the woman, even though she was the cause of these latest woes. But he loves you. You love him. You're going to have his babe this winter."

"Our love affair was ill-thought, and it is for the best that we go our separate ways. We will see each other every now and again because of his work for the Vermeals, but that can be our only contact."

"Don't you hear what our Lucinda hears from her father? The wife is comatose and has not eaten or drank for weeks now, the effects of too much opium. What will you do when he's a widower, girl? What will you do?"

"How unseemly it is for you to consider a person's death in such a way," Muireall said. "I won't discuss it with you."

"You shouldn't. You should be discussing it with him!"

"He'll need to observe mourning, and he has new employment and a daughter to consider. I'll not be any part of it."

Aunt stood, her arms shaking with the effort to push out of the chair, refusing Muireall's help. "You stubborn girl. I suppose you needed your righteousness and your backbone when raising a family as a young girl yourself, but you're only hurting yourself and Mr. Marcus and that dear Ann when you wrap yourself up in your guilt now."

"That is hardly fair. It is enough that I'm expecting a child without a husband. Mother and Father would be ashamed of me!" Muireall hissed.

"See how your misery and your guilt keep you company when you're old like me. This child," she pointed to Muireall's stomach, "will grow up and go away with their own family. Where will you be, Muireall? You'll be alone. But you'll have your piety to keep you warm."

Muireall watched Murdoch make her way into the house, shouting for Payden to come carry her chair.

ANTHONY SAT READING A DOSSIER ON A COMPANY HOPING TO manufacture treadle sewing machines for home use, although the design had been retooled several times and was set to be again, but Vermeal thought it was something to keep their eye on over the coming years. Ann was at a small table and chair he'd bought for their second-floor parlor, working on multiplication, her head bent over her paper in concentration. They'd had a fine dinner together, talking more than they had in weeks, and Ann with more smiles than he'd seen lately.

"I don't care for arithmetic, Papa," Ann said.

He sipped his coffee and looked over the top of his folder. "No?"

She shook her head. "I like books better. I like grammar class and when we get to write down our own stories."

"An authoress? Do I have an authoress on my hands?"

"Papa! Don't tease!" she said with a laugh. "Miss Painter is reading to us from a book about four sisters. It is ever so good, and everyone in class gets so very excited when she says it is time for more of Miss Alcott's story."

Anthony listened to her impassioned retelling of the book and smiled at her, at his precious girl. She was talking animatedly, as though the last month or two had not occurred and they were living in a second-floor, single room apartment above Mrs. Phillips. Without romanticizing their existence then, because they were hungry on occasion and often cold, there was a simplicity and a closeness that he was not sure could be recreated. But perhaps it was just that Ann had been younger then and he'd been desperate and tired with little adult interactions. But would he wish himself back?

Never. He was not ridiculous thinking that tasty, hearty, and regular meals were less appealing than scraping together whatever the grocer was selling cheaply and cooking it atop the heating stove in the corner of their rooms. There was no comparison between the fascinating and well-compensated work he did now and carrying deliveries for the grocer and the worry that came from thinking he mayn't even have that room for he and Ann if he was unable to earn enough coins.

She was chattering away in her lilting young girl voice, and he felt suddenly bereft of all the love he could give and receive from his unborn child and from Muireall Thompson, surely the love of his life. He did not know how to break through her guilt and worry to find themselves again in the sweet and wonderful throes of an impending "happily ever after." He could not blame her, though, could he? He was a married man.

But he would let himself dream on occasion of reuniting with her. He was not fool enough to believe there would not be troubles and arguments—there would be—but that rare jubilant anticipation that the recognition of a new love brings was gone, slipped or torn from their grasp with the violence that had nearly taken her and Ann away from this earth forever.

And now, with all the strangeness of a two-penny horror novel, he was living with his comatose wife and only pining for what might never be.

"Papa? Are you listening to me?"

"Always," he said and pulled himself upright. "I think it is time for you to put down the dreaded arithmetic and I will put down my work, and we will go to the kitchen and have a second slice of the apple pie that Mrs. Brewer made."

"Oh yes! It was delicious, and I do like a little snack before bed."

As he opened the door of the parlor, he saw Virginia's nurse hurrying to him.

"Mr. Marcus? I think you'd best come with me to Mrs. Marcus's room."

THE EARLY JUNE AIR THAT DAY WAS WARM BUT NOT OVERLY HOT after a particularly warm May. Muireall was out of the Locust Street house for an outing of pleasure, other than to visit her sisters or brother, since Plowman had taken her hostage. She had resisted all attempts to shop or step out prior to this because she had no interest in showing herself, a woman expecting a child, to the public in general, and she dreaded the idea that she'd meet someone she knew or be introduced as "Miss" Thompson with a bulging stomach that could not be hidden. But she'd been worn down by her sisters and sister-in-law for today's outing.

She was soon picked up by Lucinda in their very comfortable carriage, on their way to meet Elspeth and Kirsty at the Philadelphia Hotel dining room. Lucinda smiled at her as she was seated after Mr. Bauer had handed her inside.

"I cannot tell you how glad I am to be out of the house and out from under James's constant attentions," Lucinda said with a laugh. "Not that I usually mind, but since Maeve was born, he has gotten it in his head to carry me around in his arms, as if I am not a fully grown woman who can walk from her bed to the dining room!"

Muireall smiled and regarded Lucinda, who had been cold and standoffish when she and James had first begun dancing around each other. Her marriage, Muireall believed, and little Maeve had allowed Lucinda to find her true self, able to be less guarded in her interactions. A more unlikely pair could never be found, Muireall had thought, and Kirsty had agreed at the time, between her rambunctious, sometimes reckless, and charismatic brother and the tall, aloof Lucinda Vermeal, the object of desire of every handsome and well-situated man in the city of Philadelphia. But Elspeth had been correct. They would each soften the other's edges.

Marriage did that sometimes, especially in the best unions, Muireall thought and gazed out the window as the neighborhood houses rolled by. It made her wonder what Anthony was doing that beautiful Saturday. Was he still working or doing something special with Ann or just relaxing and perhaps reading a book? She missed him. How had she gone from viewing him as an unwelcome interloper, only tolerated for the sake of his daughter, who was the easiest child in the world to love, to feeling as if he was a part of her, of her life and future, and that there would never be another man who would mean that much to her?

"My father is worse, if it is possible," Lucinda said. "He arrived at the house this morning and told me he'd heard from his butler, Laurent, that I'd be out for a luncheon and that he could not countenance his son-in-law being left on his own to attend his granddaughter. As if there was not a wonderful and kind nurse seeing to Maeve's care when James or I must be from home."

"I imagine those two will circle each other, vying to hold little Maeve. Hopefully, they won't come to fists!" Muireall said.

"I told James that he must allow my father to fuss over her or else," Lucinda said with a small smile.

"Or else?"

Lucinda glanced out the window. "The doctor has said we may resume relations if I'm up to it. I'm quite looking forward to it, and James, is, well, James."

There was no embarrassment on Lucinda's face or in her words. That act was a part of her marriage that she clearly treasured. Muireall imagined James was impatient to renew his addresses, especially as motherhood had added a new glow and beauty to this already stunning woman, but more than any of that, he loved her desperately and she him. It made her remember that treasured afternoon where she'd given up on all of her misgivings, her worries, her long-held scruples, and given herself to Anthony Marcus. That interlude had been glorious in every possible way. She would never, ever forget the feeling of belonging and love and womanliness that she'd felt when Anthony stretched out on top of her. God, she still loved him desperately, even after going to great mental and emotional lengths to disassociate herself from him.

The carriage stopped, and Mr. Bauer opened the door and helped them both down to the walkway in front of the hotel. Muireall took a deep breath as faces and eyes turned her way. Lucinda must have noticed her hesitation and slid her arm through Muireall's, bringing her tight against her side as they climbed the wide marble steps to where a uniformed man opened the hotel doors.

"Here they are, Elspeth," Kirsty said as they approached the table in the light and airy dining room with white marble floors, masses of flowers and plants, and a hum of conversation from other guests. Muireall was soon seated after kissing both of her sisters' cheeks.

"You look well recovered from your confinement, Lucinda," Elspeth said.

"I'm feeling back to my old self, although I'm not sure my waist will ever be back to its original size," she said. "But that is an easy sacrifice to make in exchange for our Maeve."

"How are you feeling, Muireall?" Kirsty asked, and Muireall felt her cheeks burn red.

"Must we talk about it? I was really hoping to enjoy a meal with my sisters and sister-in-law without mention of my . . . predicament."

Kirsty stared at her wide-eyed and did not look away until the waiter served them all the first course, the oyster stew the hotel was famous for. "Of course. I didn't realize your coming child was a 'predicament,'" Kirsty said, her tone angry and embarrassed.

Muireall picked up her spoon and began to eat. She would not be drawn into an argument even if Kirsty was correct. She loved her coming child with every fiber of herself, even admitting her and Anthony's lovemaking may have been rash. But she just did not want to talk about all of her conflicting feelings with anyone, even with the women closest to her in every way.

Elspeth dabbed at her mouth. "Since we have been unable to discuss in any satisfactory manner your upcoming motherhood without you leaving the kitchen or the parlor or even locking yourself in your room, we've brought you to lunch in the hope that good manners, of which you are all that is correct, will keep you seated, will keep all of our voices moderated, and will allow us to discuss this sensitive subject without interruption."

Muireall felt anger rise up in her throat. She laid her damask napkin down beside her teacup and looked at Elspeth, who was staring steadily back. "You will insist on ruining this day for me. I should have stayed home."

"Please do not allow yourself to become upset." Lucinda laid a hand on her arm. "There are some things that need disc—"

"She's dead," Kirsty said.

Muireall turned quickly to her youngest sister. "Who is dead?"

"Virginia Marcus. His wife. She's dead, and he's a widower."

Muireall realized her mouth was hanging open and quickly closed it. "What happened?"

"Oh, don't be thinking she faked her own death again. I asked Albert about her, and he said she had a serious and long-standing opium addiction, from what he could tell, and when she drank all that laudanum aboard the ship her body could not handle the amount. She didn't just react in her normal way to a dose she was accustomed to. She took too much because she'd been deprived for so long, and her brain stopped working because of that. It's called a coma, where the person is alive but their brain stops working. That's what Albert said he gathered from what you said and her condition. Anyway, she'd dead."

"Virginia Marcus is dead?" she whispered.

"I must give Mr. Marcus credit for keeping her, along with a nurse, at his home after her overdose," Lucinda said. "He did not want to, according to Mr. Critchfeld. The two men have become close, and he confided that he was shocked when Mr. Marcus said she was there in a room on the third floor of the house and that she'd not awoken or even moved."

"But Mr. Marcus is an honorable man, even to the point of caring for a person who threatened everyone he loved and who'd deceived him so terribly before," Elspeth said.

"Mr. Critchfeld said that Mr. Marcus said that regardless of how they'd come to the place they were at, he'd taken a vow to care for her in sickness and in health," Lucinda said. "Not every man would be as noble considering the history between the two of them."

Muireall felt tears well in her eyes. She gulped a breath and leaned back in her chair, thankful the waiter had come to serve them steaming croquettes covered in a thick chicken-and-mushroom gravy. The smell was delicious, and she concentrated on that, on her breath going in and out of her lungs, on her fork and knife beside her plate, and of conversation swirling around the table. Elspeth, Kirsty, and Lucinda were trying their meals and saying how very delicious everything was. Muireall was nearly winning the battle of concentrating on the casual conversation instead of the details about Anthony her sisters and Lucinda had revealed.

"When did she die?" Muireall whispered, recalling that she'd sent Anthony a message to stop sending her daily notes several weeks ago. She'd thought it best. He must have assumed she did not want to hear from him any longer.

"Last Friday," Elspeth said.

"Mr. Critchfeld said he had a service for her at a nearby church and paid for her casket and all the rest of it. Mr. Critchfeld went to be supportive to Mr. Marcus, and it was just he, Mr. Critchfeld, and Ann," Lucinda said.

"I'm not sure I can stay and eat and act as if nothing has changed," Muireall said.

"Yes, you can." Kirsty patted her hand. "You are the strongest person I know or will ever know. You have managed us all at the sacrifice of yourself and your own happiness. We will stay, as you've always told us Mother would expect us to be ladies regardless of the situation. We will stay because this news is shocking. And we will stay because I'm told the patisserie makes the most delicious raspberry tarts available anywhere in the city."

Elspeth and Lucinda laughed, and Muireall couldn't stop a smile. "Oh, Kirsty, dear. You really are a treasure."

CHAPTER 17

Anthony was hardly ready to do any socializing, but Mr. Vermeal had invited some gentlemen and their wives who were on a grand tour of the United States to his home, and who also happened to own a factory in France that made stemware so fine and so intricate that their products had been declared the best in the world by persons who were qualified to know those sorts of things. He was having a cocktail and speaking to Critchfeld while Vermeal gave the guests a tour of his home.

Lucinda and James Thompson came into the room just then, apologizing for their late arrival. Critchfeld spoke to Lucinda about a project he was working on for her, and James turned to face him.

"How is little Maeve?" Anthony asked.

"She's already beautiful and a terror," James said proudly. "I'm afraid for Lucinda and I when she is seventeen or eighteen years old."

Anthony chuckled. "She'll be fine. Her parents will make sure of that."

"Like your Ann? I miss that girl. How is she doing?"

"She's well. But these last months have been hard on her."

"I'm sure. She must have been terrified when she realized what was happening," James said.

"She was. And then with . . . her mother at our house. She hadn't been sleeping well."

"Lucinda told me you had her there while she was ill," James said and accepted a glass from Laurent with a nod. "I don't know if I could have done what you did. Had her under my roof, knowing everything that she'd done. I won't speak ill of the dead, though."

"She's gone. It's a blessing. She never moved all those weeks she was there. Not a movement of a finger or a twitch, although her eyes opened at the end."

"Were you with her?"

He nodded. "As much as I resented her, even hated her for the trouble and the deceit, I couldn't bring myself to let her die alone, with only a stranger in the room. I dismissed the nurse and sat with her after she told me Virginia had started breathing strangely. She passed sometime after midnight that night."

James took a deep swallow of whatever dark liquid was in his crystal glass. "So you're a widower now."

"And this time I'm certain of it." He hesitated, looking at the ice swirling in his own glass. "How is she? She told me to stop sending her messages."

"My sister is the most stubborn, unbending woman to have ever been born. She's also been the rock of our family, who have survived and thrived in spite of being parentless and in danger. She's embarrassed now, I think. But she's got to get over whatever misgivings she may have, and you do too. There's a lad or a lass to consider."

"She doesn't want anything to do with me, I don't think."

James laughed and held up his empty glass to the young man serving drinks. "Then you'll have to convince her otherwise."

He could not stop thinking about what James had said to him even as he struggled to understand the broken English of the young woman seated beside him at dinner. His French was rusty from the last time he'd studied it during his schooling fifteen years prior, and it was doing him little good now.

* * *

ANN WAS IN THE BACKYARD OF THE HOUSE, HELPING REYNOLDS rake the leaves on a sunny September day. Anthony was watching her through the window of his study, working and talking to his coachman, who was not replying all that much to anything Ann was saying. He opened the window and called to her.

"Would you like to take a walk to the park? We can see if the festival is still going on there," he called down.

"Mr. Reynolds and I are not finished with the raking, Papa."

"You never mind, Miss Ann. I'll be fine on my own," Reynolds said and took the rake from her hands.

Ann hurried inside, and Anthony went down the steps to the front door. They walked together to the park, down the tree-lined street, past some new homes being built. The air was crisp, even cool, and they kicked leaves with their boots as they walked.

"Winter will be here before we know it," he said.

"I think it will be very different, though, from last winter, don't you? We are never out of coal anymore."

He laughed. "No, we are not." Anthony was proud of himself when he considered his finances from last year to now. He'd saved much of his monthly pay every time he received it, paying for whatever supplies his household needed, Ann's tuition, new clothing when necessary, and lately, the expense of Virginia's nursing and her funeral. But even that amount did not put a large dent into his savings. He imagined most people who made what he did in salary attended operas and expensive entertainments and visited resorts and such. He did none of that and had a fat bank account to show for it, although he must contrive a way to pay for the expenses of his and Muireall's child when he or she were born.

"Could we go visit the sisters and Mrs. Phillips soon?" Ann asked, breaking into his thoughts.

"We can. I've been meaning to make a donation to the orphanage for some time. We'll plan on visiting soon."

"We could take a fancy cake for Mrs. Phillips from the bakery that Mrs. Brewer buys from sometimes."

"She would like that, wouldn't she?"

"She would," Ann said and looked up at him. "And while we are in that part of town, we could stop and see Miss Thompson. I would like that very much, Papa. Wouldn't you?"

"Miss Thompson did not return any of the messages I sent nearly daily for more than a month while she recovered her health. She has not replied to me. It is not fair to her to keep pressing my attentions there." He said glanced down at Ann now that he'd said the speech he'd been planning in anticipation of these questions from her. She stared back at him, her mouth, her eyes troubled and bright with tears.

"She does not love us anymore?" she asked softly.

He stopped, crouched down, and turned her to him on the wide tree-lined avenue where they walked. "I believe she will always love you. I'm sure of it."

"But she doesn't want us?"

"It's me she doesn't want. It's a grown-up subject, but we were to marry, as you know, and then it was discovered I was still married to your mother. It was a very difficult situation for her."

Ann looked up and down the street until her eyes finally came to rest on his. "My feet are aching in these shoes, Papa. Can we just go home? I don't want to go to the festival any longer."

Anthony stood, bent down, and picked her up.

"Papa! You will hurt your leg," she said even as she clung to him and buried her face in his shoulder.

"Don't you worry about your papa. I'll get us where we need to go. Haven't I always?" he asked, holding her tight against his chest.

She nodded, and he could feel her sobs against his neck.

* * *

"MR. MARCUS?" ANTHONY'S NEW SECRETARY SAID WHEN HE opened the door to the library at the Vermeal mansion.

Anthony looked up as Mr. Vermeal fell silent in the discussion they were having about Critchfeld's looming retirement. "Yes, Mr. Hinton?" he asked a bit impatiently. "What is it?"

"Well, sir, there's a young woman here. She's insisting on . . ."

"Mr. Marcus! Mr. Marcus?" he heard from the hallway. He stood quickly and went to the door.

"Sarah? What is it?" he said, feeling the bite of terror at his back. The maid was tearful and red-faced.

"I'm so sorry, sir, but Mrs. Smithy said I was to talk to you right away and not to let anyone stand in me way."

The air he was breathing felt cold suddenly, and his fingertips were tingling. It was as if he'd been thrown back to a scene at the Pendergast home several months ago when Sarah had delivered some devastating news to him.

"Go ahead, Sarah. Tell me what is the matter," he said and noticed Mr. Vermeal and Critchfeld had come to stand behind him.

"It is Miss Ann, sir," she said, and he felt himself stagger. Critchfeld put an arm through his, holding him straight. If he hadn't, Anthony thought he may have fallen to the floor.

"Tell us, girl," Mr. Vermeal said. "Don't keep your employer waiting."

"Oh yes, sir. The thing is Mr. Reynolds picked up Miss Ann at school, like he always does, and when he stopped at the carriage house to unhitch the horse, he told Miss Ann to go on in the back door, that Duke was favoring his front hoof and he wanted to check it. He told her Mrs. Brewster had oatmeal biscuits hot from the oven ready for her, to go on inside," the girl said and stopped to draw breath. "But she didn't."

"Ann didn't go inside? Where did she go?" he asked, feeling the urge to shake the girl by the shoulders.

"We don't know. Mr. Reynolds came in the house some thirty minutes later, Mrs. Brewster figured, and Mrs. Smithy asked where Miss Ann was. He thought she'd gone in the house, but she didn't."

"Hinton? My coat, please," he said as Vermeal shouted to his butler to get the gig out front immediately.

"Do you want me to come?" Critchfeld asked.

He shook his head. "I would appreciate it, though, if you would check with Mr. Pendergast or Mr. Thompson and make sure that Plowman fellow hasn't reappeared on the scene. I don't think that is what happened, but I don't know for sure. I do know that Ann has been despondent. She is hiding, I fear."

Anthony arrived home to a white-faced Reynolds and an openly weeping Mrs. Smithy. "You've checked her room? Is everything still in place?"

"Everything is just as I left it after straightening her room after she left for school this morning. We've looked everywhere, sir."

Reynolds swallowed. "I can't tell you how sorry I am that I didn't walk that child to the door. If you're aiming to get rid of me, I'll go now, but I'd like to help with the search before I leave."

"You're not going anywhere, Reynolds," he said and turned to Sarah when she came in the kitchen.

"Here's a message for you, sir," she said.

He opened it, read the message, and closed his eyes. He had a feeling where his daughter had gone. "There seems to be no more threat from the men from earlier this year, according to Mr. Pendergast. I think I know where she went, but I can't figure out how she got there," he said as much to himself as to his staff assembled in front of him. "How would an eight-year-old get to the other side of the river and beyond?"

"Ah, sir," Sarah said. "Miss Ann asked me how I got myself to me mum's house on my day out, and I told her I went with friends that work nearby and live near me mum, but if they weren't going then I took the trolley if I had a spare penny."

"The trolley?"

"Miss Ann was right interested about where I caught it and how long it took and how I figured out which stop to get off the first time I took it."

"What did you tell her, Sarah?" Anthony asked.

"I told her I just asked the driver, and he told me what street to listen for when they hollered the stops."

"Reynolds, is Duke fit to ride?"

"Yes, sir. Just had a stone under his shoe. He's right as rain now."

"Would you saddle him for me and tell Mr. Vermeal's groom that he needn't wait any longer? I'll ride to where I need to go. Thank you all for your diligence. I'll bring our girl home, but she will be having no dessert for weeks for causing us all this worry!"

Muireall climbed the steps from the canning kitchen in the cellar of the Locust Street house. She was tired and filthy after washing, peeling, and canning bushels of Chambersburg peaches and apples over the last few days with Mrs. McClintok, Payden, and Robbie. Mrs. McClintok had come up ahead of her while the boys cleaned up to begin dinner.

"Let me wash up a bit, Mrs. McClintok, and then I'll get the potatoes started."

She climbed the next flight of steps to her room, thinking that every ounce this child increased made her flight to the second floor take a minute or two longer. Thankfully, there was still wash water in the pitcher. She took off her dress and washed under her arms and breasts and over her bulging stomach. A glance in the mirror revealed her bed behind her, where it had all happened. Where Anthony had touched her and she'd touched him and they'd made love and made this child.

Muireall heard a knock at the front door and hurried to fasten the top button of her dress. Had it been any member of the family, they would have just come in and not knocked. She opened her bedroom door and called down to the kitchen. "I'll see who is here."

She pulled the door open and looked down as the person on the stoop was not an adult. It was an eight-year-old. Ann Marcus. Her heart constricted at the sight of her. As the girl meant to be her very own daughter and whom she loved.

Muireall looked out the door, up and down the street. "Ann, dear. Where is your father?"

"May I come in, Miss Thompson?"

"Of course," she said and opened the door wide. "But who are you with?"

"I'm by myself. I took the trolley," she said. "I had to see you."

"Ann..."

"I know Papa will be worried and furious. I don't care anymore. I've asked to visit you, and he will not bring me. He says you don't want us anymore, and I want to know why."

"Your father will be panicked! Oh, Ann!"

"I just want to know why," Ann said, tears rolling down her cheeks. "What have I done? Why don't you love us anymore?"

Muireall closed the door and took Ann by the hand to the parlor. She sat on a chair by the fireplace and pulled Ann on her lap, although it was a tight squeeze, and wrapped an arm around her. Ann laid her hand on Muireall's stomach.

"Is there a baby in there? Did you get married to some other man?"

"There is a baby in there, and that child is your father's child too," Muireall said, wondering how to explain it all to a young child. An innocent child.

"But you are not married," Ann said, looking bewildered. "The sisters told me that when a man and a woman love each other, they get married, and sometimes God gives them a baby. Do you love Papa?"

And that really was the crux of the matter. How could she lie to this precious girl? But how could she begin to explain the conflicting feelings in her heart and mind? How to tell her that she was clinging to the memory of her parents, long dead now, who would have only wished for her happiness in any way she sought it, but who she was still, fifteen years later, trying to emulate and portend what their reaction might be? How did she explain that by denying her heart, she was attempting to honor a code that could not guide her?

She could feel tears well in her eyes. "Yes. Of course I love your papa. Every bit as much as I love you."

Ann laid her head on Muireall's breast, patted her stomach, and closed her eyes. Muireall smiled, a weepy, trembling one, but the first true one she'd smiled in months. She kissed Ann's hair and closed her eyes, exhaustion claiming her. She did not rest long, though. The pounding on the front door and Mrs. McClintok's hurried trip to answer it woke her.

"Oh, Mr. Marcus," Muireall heard the housekeeper say, but he did not wait to hear anything else she might have said.

"Ann! Ann! Are you here?" Anthony shouted. "Ann!"

"Papa! I am here, Papa!" she said as she wiggled off Muireall's lap.

He came into the room, breathing hard, looking as if he were an avenging lord in his tall hat and dark coat and reminding her of the first time he'd come searching for his daughter, although he'd gained weight and confidence since that day. He went down on one knee, and his daughter flew to him, and he hugged her to his chest. He set her back from him and held her face in his hands.

"Do you have any idea how many people are worried about you? I'm angry but so happy to have found you."

"I am truly sorry, Papa. I will apologize and do extra chores if you'd like. But I had to talk to her, to Miss Thompson," she said.

Anthony pulled himself to his feet and took Ann by the hand. "Say good-bye now. We don't want to trouble Miss Thompson any more than we already have," he said and swung his eyes to Muireall. "You are looking remarkably well, if I might say so. I hope you are feeling well too."

Muireall stood and walked to him. "I am feeling well, and thank you for asking. Ann is never trouble for me. I love her."

Anthony nodded, tight-lipped. He was prepared to walk away from her, she could tell. He was prepared to sacrifice his wants and needs for her happiness. Because she knew he still loved her. There was something in his eyes that had betrayed those finer feelings since not long after they had met. She wondered if she was as readable to him.

"I've been so very foolish, Anthony," she said and smiled. She looked down at Ann. "Mrs. McClintok has much to do to get dinner ready, dear. Would you go help her, please?"

Ann looked from one to the other and hurried away.

"What . . . what have you been foolish about, Miss Thompson?" he said as he twirled his hat in his hands.

"I will tell you all of it sometime later, but for now, I must tell you that I love you. I have loved you since you first ate dinner with us in the dining room, even though I could never have identified it as love at the time. I'm so terribly sorry. I've hurt you. I've hurt Ann. Please, Anthony . . ."

And then she was in his arms, and he was kissing her and holding her tight to him, and his eyes were shining with unshed tears while hers coursed down her cheeks.

"My dearest. I love you so very much, and I am free to say that now. Virginia Marcus passed away."

"I know. My sisters and Lucinda told me," she said, and

touched his face. "It may seem wrong to say, but you have my sympathy."

He kissed her fingertips. "It is strange to think, because I believed her dead all these years, and with all the trouble and danger she caused for you and for Ann, that I would feel anything but anger and relief. And I do feel both of those things, but there is some sorrow as well for Ann's mother, regardless of her poor judgment during her life."

"I am not going to say I'm glad she is dead, but I will say I am most pleased that you are widower."

He smiled and kissed her then, like she remembered and dreamed of.

CHAPTER 18

Muireall looked at Anthony as he stood in front of the massive marble fireplace in the parlor of Elspeth and Alexander's home. It was her wedding day. The sun was shining on that fall day, filling the room with light. Their guests were seated on couches and settees and extra chairs that had been brought into the room for the occasion. James and Payden, both in their Taviston plaid, walked her from the door of the room to Anthony, where he stood waiting silently by the minister, his hand propped on his cane. She stopped her procession to kiss Aunt Murdoch, who was smiling and holding a sleeping Maeve in her arms.

"Rory and Cullodena are watching you today with love. You've made every dream they had for you come true, *mo ghradh*," she whispered to Muireall.

Muireall walked the rest of the way with her eyes on Anthony. What had she been thinking to believe that she could spend her life separate from him? She'd always been so proud of the Taviston title and the Thompson name they'd adopted when they'd arrived on these shores all those years ago, but she thought becoming Mrs. Muireall Marcus would be the wisest and kindest thing she'd ever done for herself.

"Who gives the bride this day?" the minister asked.

"Her brothers," they said and each kissed her cheek as James moved her hand from his arm to Anthony's fingers.

She smiled up at Anthony, feeling loved and beautiful in her new pale blue dress and darker blue jacket with a high collar that framed her face and the soft rolls of her hair and, of course, her mother's plaid over her shoulder and pinned with a jeweled clasp at her hip. The minister spoke the sacred words that bound them together for all time. When he turned them to her friends and relatives as a married couple, she reached for Ann, who was sitting between Elspeth and Mrs. Phillips, Anthony's old landlady. Ann hurried the few steps and wrapped her arms around Muireall, laying her head against her swollen stomach.

She looked out at those assembled, smiling broadly after Anthony kissed her and the top of Ann's head. All of her family were there, her sisters and brothers and wives and husbands and children. Mr. Vermeal, Mr. Critchfeld, and all the staff from Anthony's home, Lucinda's Aunt Louisa and her husband and daughter, several nuns from the orphanage, Mrs. McClintok beside Mr. Bamblebit, MacAvoy and Eleanor, Alexander's parents and his sister, Annabelle. Even Lady Watson, Albert's mother, had condescended to attend a wedding that was not held in a church, as was proper, she'd told Kirsty. Everyone near and dear to her was there, and the dearest to her at her side, Anthony and Ann.

THEY'D DONE IT, ANTHONY THOUGHT AS HE KISSED Muireall's fingers. They'd done it, and he admitted it had been no small feat to bring the two of them together, from his poverty to her obligations, with the reappearance of his dead wife and danger to them all. He would have his family, finally, in a clean, orderly home with staff to see to their needs and money for necessities and pleasures too. He loved her beyond measure. He wondered if she would welcome his attentions in the bedroom, although he was prepared to wait for whenever she was comfortable and able to make love to him.

The luncheon had been delicious and perfectly handled by his sister-in-law's staff. Muireall was glowing beside him, eating small bites and sipping her champagne between glancing at him and touching his arm. It must have felt just as unreal to her as it did to him.

He'd written his aunt and uncle about his marriage, and they planned to travel to Philadelphia in the spring to meet Muireall and the new child. They hadn't seen Ann since she was very small. His sister and her husband would come at the same time. What an event that would be! He intended to open his small ballroom and host his family and hers for a party. He must tell his wife—his wife!—of his plans. He could no longer make household and family decisions on his own, and he was very glad of it.

He joined her as she circulated among the tables, speaking to each person in her gracious and ladylike way. If he had not known she was the daughter of the Earl and Countess of Taviston, he would have still known she had centuries of well-mannered behavior in her breeding and ancestry. She was generous and loving and beautiful and, most importantly, his. By midafternoon, he could tell she was tiring. He asked Elspeth to get her sister's gloves and hat.

Anthony tapped on his wineglass with his spoon and waited until the room quieted. "I want to thank every one of you for all your support and care of my lovely bride over the last few months and for your attendance today to celebrate our marriage with us. I especially want to thank the Pendergasts for opening their home and providing us with a delicious meal. But now I plan to whisk her away for a short honeymoon."

He held out his hand to her, and she came to him, smiling and blushing. She kissed Aunt Murdoch and her sisters and sister-in-law on her way to him. Then she stopped and knelt before Ann, who was staying with the Pendergasts for the few days they'd be gone. Elspeth had a trundle bed set up in Aunt Murdoch's room, where Ann had asked to sleep. His wife and daughter hugged and kissed, and then she was at his side, his beautiful bride.

"WHERE ARE WE GOING, HUSBAND?" SHE ASKED AND LAID HER head on his shoulder once they were in the carriage.

"To the Philadelphia Hotel, the most exclusive, fanciest room they have. They have a little orchestra that will play near the dining room tonight, and we can eat and talk alone, which we don't always have a chance to do, and of which we will have less of a chance once this new child arrives. But I thought first you could use a nap."

"Oh, Anthony. That all sounds wonderful, especially the nap." She laughed.

The hotel staff was especially accommodating, remarking that Mr. Vermeal himself had arranged for their stay. Their rooms on the seventh floor had a sitting room with fresh flowers and chilling champagne and a sleeping room with a massive bed and their clothes already hanging in the closet. The hotel manager accompanied them and said that coffee, tea, and light refreshments had been ordered and they had but to ring the bell and it would all be brought.

"My wife has had a long day, and she may want to retire for a while. I'll ring when we are ready for it," Anthony said and handed the man a folded bill.

"My husband is quite the man about town, tipping the manager of the hotel so slyly," she said as she unpinned her hat.

"I'm quite the sophisticate. Just ask my landlady, Mrs. Phillips," he said and smiled at her.

She laughed, as he'd surely intended, and went into the bedroom. "I'm going to rest."

He kissed her forehead and closed the bedroom door behind her. She managed to undress herself down to her lace-edged silk shift. She imagined Anthony would need some prodding and climbed under the covers.

"Anthony?" she called, and he rushed into the room. She saw that he'd loosened his tie, taken off his jacket, and rolled up his sleeves, revealing his muscled forearms. He was wholly desirable.

"What is it? Are you well?"

"I'm well, husband. I'm wondering why you are still in the sitting room and not in here with me."

He sat on the edge of the bed. "I wanted to let you rest."

She sat up, the sheet dropping to her waist, leaving her bare but for her silk chemise that barely covered her breasts. His eyes scanned her, and he looked up, regretfully, she thought, and cleared his throat.

"Muireall," he whispered. "We can wait. There is no rush, darling."

She felt her face color. "I asked Dr. Gibson if it was safe to make love, and he said it was as long as I was comfortable."

"You asked a doctor?"

"I couldn't ask Albert," she said. "I just couldn't bring the subject up with him. Dr. Gibson was recommended by Lucinda and has been caring for our family for several years."

"I don't suppose you could ask your brother-in-law."

She shook her head and unbuttoned the top of his shirt, pulling his tie from under his collar. "Would you like to have a rest too?" she said, looking at him from under her lashes.

"I would," he said and stripped down to his short drawers. She drew in a breath as he walked to his side of the bed, all long muscular limbs, his chest and legs covered in dark hair. He pulled her into his arms and kissed her, slipping his tongue into her mouth, tasting her, and stretching his hand down her side. Her breasts were sensitive and pressed tightly against his chest, making her hum with need.

"I've dreamt of this, Anthony. Of that magical afternoon when we made this child. I wanted you then," she said and pulled his hand to her breast, making them both groan. "And I want you as much, if not more, now. My stomach is stretched, and my body isn't as shapely . . ."

"My God, Muireall. Your body is perfect. Your breasts are heavy and full in my hand, and this child," he touched her belly, reverently, "makes you more desirable to me, not less. Come atop me, my love."

He rolled onto his back, and Muireall soon understood that this position would be more comfortable for them both. She pulled her chemise over her head and straddled him. She closed her eyes and moved until his sex was against hers, slowly moving down over him until he was fully seated inside her, her thighs touching his hips. They both moaned.

Muireall bent over him, placing her hands on either side of his shoulders, and began to move. He touched her breasts, bringing one to his mouth to lick and suck, and played with the other as she undulated on him, bringing herself to a place where time and situation no longer existed. Just he and her, bound together where pleasure ruled. She heard him cry out, closed her eyes, and let herself find the whirlwind they'd made.

She laid down at his side and drifted off to sleep.

MUIREALL HAD JUST GOTTEN ANN IN THE CARRIAGE WITH Reynolds for school when a messenger came to the door. She was settling into being mistress of Anthony's home, getting to know Mrs. Smithy and Mrs. Brewster. She was accustomed to doing much of the household work, as she'd done on Locust Street with Mrs. McClintok, but she was glad that someone else was cleaning the floors and windows and baking the bread. Anthony had insisted she rest much of the day as she was far along in her pregnancy and tired much of the time anyway. Apparently, the most stressful thing she was permitted was to go to luncheons with

Elspeth since Lucinda was at Vermeal Industries many days and Kirsty was at her shop.

She would have to find something to do with her time, even after the baby was born, as she would be accompanying Anthony to some dinners and entertainments. She supposed she'd have to hire a nurse. Muireall had found herself in the strange situation of being a society wife.

Mrs. Smithy handed her an envelope.

"Thank you, Mrs. Smithy," she said and glanced at the envelope. It was from Scotland. "I'll read this in the parlor."

Muireall had received regular updates over the years from the Court of the Lord Lyon, but it had been nearly a year since she'd received one, she thought after a moment, thinking of what had been in that missive. She sat down, opened the envelope, read, and groaned aloud. There would have to be a family meeting. She went to her desk to begin notes to her sisters and brothers to join her and Anthony for dinner the following evening. She'd best let Mrs. Brewster and Mrs. Smithy know there would be ten for dinner plus Ann and a few infants.

* * *

JAMES PUSHED HIMSELF BACK FROM THE TABLE AND RUBBED HIS stomach. "That was all delicious. I'll make a point of stopping to compliment your cook."

"Yes. Everything was very good," Elspeth added.

Kirsty turned to Muireall. "Is there some special occasion we are unaware of? It's just been a week since your wedding, and we're all gathered together again. Not that Albert or I mind a bit."

Muireall picked up the letter lying beside her plate and unfolded the paper. "I wanted us all together to hear what the Lyon Clerk at the Court of the Lord Lyon has said."

"The Lyon Clerk?" Alexander asked.

"The Court of the Lord Lyon is where disputes of the nature of ours with Plowman are settled as well as requests for new coats of arms and recordkeeping. I have communicated with him over the years as the earl's guardian," she said and nodded at Payden. "He has kept me abreast of what is happening with Plowman's case, of which he has no legal standing, and also of what is occurring at Dunacres."

"What does the letter say?" Elspeth asked.

Muireall took a deep breath and glanced around the table. "It says that Plowman lives."

"What! No!" James shouted.

"I thought I had him," Anthony murmured.

"Will this never be over?" Kirsty whispered.

Aunt Murdoch cleared her throat. "Not until that murderer is dead and in his grave, a knife through that blackguard's heart."

"He says Plowman is badly injured and recovering at an unknown address, but he has it on reliable authority that his health is not good. He will keep us abreast of anything else he hears."

The table was quiet, Anthony staring steadily at her. She knew what he was thinking without him saying a word. He would guard her and his family with his life, and she knew that to be true. She would not live in fear, but they all must continue to be cautious. Forever, it seemed.

Mrs. Smithy bustled in just then, clearing plates as Mrs. Brewster served chocolate cake with caramel icing. Everyone ate in silence, knowing the gravity of Plowman being alive to continue his torments.

"I'm going to speak to Graham, the head of Pendergast security, about what we can do to minimize threats. He will most likely want to speak to each of you and see your homes to give us a fair assessment. If everyone's in agreement, of course," Alexander said.

James, Albert, and Anthony all agreed to give tours of their properties as well as the homestead on Locust Street.

"The clerk said he would alert us as he hears of Plowman's recovery or demise and if he travels to America again," she said.

It was not long until her sisters and brothers took their leave, after quiet good-byes.

* * *

MUIREALL WAS UP EARLY THE FOLLOWING TUESDAY, INTENT ON finding out from her youngest brother why he and Robbie had not shown themselves at her home to help her with cleaning the attics with Mrs. Smithy the day before. There were several heavy, old trunks and some furniture, including a sturdy table and chairs, that she thought the orphanage could use or give to families in need. She and Mrs. Smithy and Sarah had wrapped hankies around their faces to guard from dust and sorted through several generations of clothing, books, and even some memorabilia from the War of 1812 left over from one owner of the house to the next. She thought one of the city's museums may be interested in some of those items. They collected barrels of trash for the refuse man, and she gave Sarah several bolts of cloth that were at least twenty years old but in relatively good shape.

As Reynolds drove her to Locust Street on that beautiful October day, she recalled with a smile how angry Anthony had been when he came home from work and found her dressed in old, filthy clothes, her hair tied on her head with a scarf. She had been in the bathing chamber when he came into the room, railing at her that she must take better care of herself and that she was not under any circumstance to do the heavy work she'd done that day ever again. She'd slowly removed her clothing, sneezing a few times, and laughing because of it, while her husband's ranting died to a whimper of lust.

She'd bathed, he'd dried her, slowly and carefully, and carried her to their bedroom, leaving the room for a moment to call down to Mrs. Smithy that they would be late for dinner and would she please get Ann started on her homework. What followed had been glorious and reminded her she was the luckiest woman alive.

She climbed the steps to the Locust Street house, used her key in the lock, and called for Mrs. McClintok as she removed her coat and hat.

"Ah, Muireall, you're looking well, but don't come near me," the housekeeper said from the kitchen doorway. "I've caught a cold and don't want you to have it too."

"Do you have any willow bark here?" Muireall asked. "I can smell something baking. You should be lying down if you're not well."

"I intend to as soon as I pull the bread from the oven."

"Where are the boys?" Muireall asked, thinking she'd best not call the two strapping young men boys much longer.

"They went to an event at Mr. Thompson's gymnasium last night and left early to meet with some other young men. They told me they'd be home late and that they had their keys. Truthfully, Muireall, I was feeling so ill I went to bed before the sun went down and didn't wake until just an hour ago. I can't remember ever sleeping that late in all of my life!"

Muireall laughed. "No one deserves some extra rest more than you. I want you to bring Mr. Bamblebit to dinner some evening next week when he can be away from work and you're feeling better. Mrs. Brewster is a good cook, but not as good as you, but if we don't have to prepare it and clean up afterward, I think it will be delicious!"

Mrs. McClintok laughed. "You're right about that! If you don't mind, would you wake the boys while I finish this bread? I have a feeling they may have had a brew on their way home."

Muireall shook her head and smiled as she climbed the steps. She could hardly be angry with either of them. They both worked hard with the canning business, at Kirsty's shop on occasion, and even at James's gymnasium, which seemed to fascinate Robbie. They'd both kept up with their schooling and would be well able to attend college if they wanted. She loved them both. She rapped on Payden's door and called to him, hoping Robbie was in there sleeping too, as he often did, so she would not have to climb any more steps.

There was no answer, and she knocked again, calling their names.

"Payden? I hope you are decently covered because I'm coming in," she said loudly at the door before turning the knob. But what she saw was not what she expected. There was no eighteen-year-old young man wrapped up in a sheet, snoring and covering his head with his pillow. The bed had not been slept in. She went up the steps at the end of the hall, calling to Robbie. His room was empty as well. Surely there was a reasonable explanation, but that did not stop her stomach from rolling uncomfortably in fright. She hurried as best she could back down the steps to Payden's room.

And that's when she saw the letter on his desk with her name on it. She picked it up with shaking fingers and sat down on the bed.

To my family and Mrs. McClintok,

The news that Plowman lives, and will yet endanger us in the future, has forced my hand. By the time anyone reads this, I will be on a steamer heading across the Atlantic, to Dunacres or wherever Plowman's trail takes me. I intend to end his threats. Permanently, just as Aunt described. Do not be angry or afraid. It is my birthright and my obligation to confront those who threaten the MacTavish clan and any others in my care. I will avenge our parents' deaths, the suffering of my sisters, and the risks my brother and brothers-in-law were forced to take to defend our family.

Robbie is with me. He is not convinced of my plan, but there was never a more devoted friend, or second-in-command, than he. Please tell his mother not to worry. We will take good care of each other.

I will do what needs to be done out of love, for Muireall, more a mother than a sister, for Elspeth, the mediator, for Kirsty, my sister in mischief, for Murdoch, who knows all my secrets, and for my brother, James, the bravest of heroes. I know our expanded family, including Anthony, Lucinda, Albert, Alexander, and Mr. Bamblebit too, if Robbie and I are not mistaken, will support each of you while we are away. We will be victorious and relieve us of the daily fear that has haunted this family for nearly twenty years.

I imagine we may be gone for some time. We will write as we can and keep you informed of where we are. I have taken monies from our joint family accounts as well as my own savings to finance this trip and some items from the attic that James had squirrelled away. There is a folded note, as you see, from Robbie for his mother. I love you all more than I can write and recognize how fortunate I've been to be born into this family and raised by such extraordinary men and women.

W*ITH MY LOVE AND GRATITUDE,*
   The Tenth Earl of Taviston
   Payden MacTavish Thompson

AFTERWORD

I hope you have enjoyed Muireall and Anthony's story, the fourth in the *Thompsons of Locust Street* series. The first book in the *Thompsons of Locust Street* series is *The Bachelor's Bride*, followed by *The Bareknuckle Groom,* and *The Professor's Lady*.

Other American set historical romance series:

The Crawford Family Series includes *Train Station Bride, Contract to Wed*, companion novella, *The Maid's Quarters*, and *Her Safe Harbor* and tell the tales of three Boston sisters, heiresses to the family banking fortune.

The Gentry's of Paradise chronicle the lives of Virginia horse breeders and begins with Beauregard and Eleanor Gentry's story, set in 1842, in the prequel novella, *Into the Evermore*. The full-length novels are set in the 1870's of the next generation of Gentrys and include *For the Brave, For This Moment,* and *For Her Honor*.

Reader favorites *Romancing Olive* and *Reconstructing Jackson* are American set Prairie Romances and *Cross the Ocean i*s set in both England and America.

Politics & Bedfellows and *All the News* are my general fiction titles published under Hollis Bush.

AFTERWORD

Please leave a review where you purchased *The Captain's Woman* or on GoodReads or other social sites for readers. Thank you so much for your purchase. I love to hear from readers! Please follow me on FaceBook, Twitter, or on my website hollybushbooks.com, for book announcements. The first few pages of *Into the Evermore* and *The Bachelor's Bride* follows.

All the best,
Holly

EXCERPT FROM THE BACHELOR'S BRIDE

Chapter One

"No! No, you will not, James."

"I will do as I wish," he thundered, slamming his hand on the thick wooden table, making the crockery dance.

"I am the head of this family, and I say you will not breathe a word of this to our brother or sisters," Muireall Thompson said through gritted teeth.

"Head of the family, are you, lass?"

"I am the oldest."

"And a *real* sibling to boot," James said and marched out of the kitchen.

Elspeth hunched under the stairwell outside the kitchens and watched her brother hurry past, his leather boots slapping against the stone floors, nearly masking his whispered curse words. He slammed the door at the top of the steps. She jumped when Aunt Murdoch spoke to her, just inches from her ear.

"What are you doing, child?" she asked.

"I was eavesdropping on an argument between Muireall and James."

"Does anything good ever come from eavesdropping?"

"Nay. Never," Elspeth said. "But that won't stop me from doing it."

One side of Aunt's mouth turned up. "There's no denying you're a MacTavish, with that sassy tongue of yours."

"MacTavish, Aunt? I've heard you call one of us that on occasion, but I never understood why. Are they our ancestors? A clan we'd best forget?"

"Shush," Aunt Murdoch hissed. "Have you finished the mending? Or are you just lazing about, listening to others' private talks?"

Elspeth looked into Aunt Murdoch's filmy blue eyes. There were some mysteries surrounding her family, the Thompsons. Some secrets. She'd overheard snippets over the years as some had not realized she was in the same room with them, but lips immediately clenched when they did realize, or when her younger sister, Kirsty, or her younger brother, Payden, were nearby. Aunt knew all the secrets, she was certain, but she was just as certain that she would never reveal any of them.

"I need more blue thread to fix one of Kirsty's church dresses. I'll be going to Mrs. Fendale's for more."

"Then get there and get back," Aunt said and went through the door to the kitchens, no doubt to harass Muireall.

Elspeth found James in the parlor, repairing the floor where a nail had come up through one of the varnished boards.

"If you pound that any harder, you're going to fall through," she said, wondering what he could have possibly meant by *real sibling* when he was arguing with Muireall.

"Better than fighting with our sister," he said, each word punctuated by a pound of the hammer. He sat back on his heels and looked up at her as she pulled on her short linen jacket. "Where are you off to?"

"Mrs. Fendale's for thread."

"You shouldn't be going to that part of town alone," James said as he stood. "I have to see about this beet delivery today, but I'll take you tomorrow."

"I'll be fine, James," she said to his sputtering. She stopped at the front door and pulled on her bonnet, examining herself in the mirror above the marble table. James was still telling her she wasn't allowed to leave without him, as she was a stubborn and foolish girl, when she pulled the door closed behind her.

She set out north toward the edge of Society Hill where they lived, crossing Chestnut Street, enjoying the spring air. Streets were crowded with carriages and wagons and horses, and all types of people too. Elspeth's family knew their neighbors, and she waved at old Mrs. Cartwright sweeping her steps and watched Mr. Abrams shaking his finger at his children as their heads nodded in agreement. The sun was shining, one of the first March days to be warm, and it seemed as though everyone was out of their homes and enjoying the weather after a particularly long and cold winter.

Three blocks more and she was less likely to wave or shout a hallo. She stared straight ahead, glimpsing the swinging sign over the door of her destination, and did not listen to the ridiculous and inappropriate comments some young men were directing at her. In just their shirtsleeves, no jacket or four-in-hand tie, and even some without a vest, they were hanging about a stairwell to a basement or coal chute or leaning against the gas streetlight posts, hooting and hollering at each other and at others on the street. Once she crossed Arch Street into Southwark, the houses were a little shabby, the streets had a little more garbage strewn about, and the residents looked a little more downtrodden, but she could see Mrs. Fendale's Millinery shop, not half a block away.

Unfortunately, she'd have to pass the bawdy house—not that she was supposed to know it was a bawdy house or even know what a bawdy house was, but she did have ears and a brain between them and would have been hard-pressed not to understand the conversation she'd overheard between James and his friend MacAvoy. But as it was just ten in the morning, hopefully those ladies would still be abed. It was quiet as she passed by, with one lone woman hanging out a second-floor window in a sheer chemise, one shoulder strap hanging down her arm, with a shiny corset over top of it, which was scandalous enough, but it was red—bright, blood red! All satin and lace and nothing like her own white cotton undergarments. She wondered why a woman would want to wear such a thing, but then, with a second glance at the woman, now smiling at her and tapping a thin cigar against the brick sill, she knew. It would entice a man, but what kind? Surely not a good one! Elspeth shivered and hurried her steps.

A bell rang over her head as she entered the seamstress's shop. "Hello, Mrs. Fendale! How are you this beautiful spring day?"

"Miss Thompson! How good to see you after this long winter! What may I help you with? A new hat, perhaps?"

Elspeth shook her head. "Oh no. I'm just doing some mending and have run out of blue thread." She ran her fingertips over lace lying out on the glass-top counter. "How beautiful! Maybe I will take a yard or two of this to add to Kirsty's best dress."

"It's a very lovely lace, made right here in our neighborhood," Mrs. Fendale said with a smile. "How much shall I cut for you?"

"I think two yards. It will be perfect to liven up one of last year's dresses."

While Mrs. Fendale tied the cut ends of the lace and wrapped the purchases, her son Ezra came out from between the dark hanging curtains that led to the back of the shop where the seamstresses and hatmakers worked. His head dipped into a nod as he smiled shyly, and a blush crept up his face.

"Good morning, Ezra." Elspeth smiled at the younger man.

"G-G-Good morning, Miss Thompson," he said and swallowed.

"Here, Ezra." Mrs. Fendale handed her packages to him. "Carry Miss Thompson's things for her until she crosses the street."

EXCERPT FROM THE BACHELOR'S BRIDE

"I'll be fine, Mrs. Fendale. No need to take Ezra away from whatever work he's doing for you."

"His work will still be here when he returns, and I'll feel better knowing he's with you until you've passed this block," she said and shook her head. "To think that those hussies ply . . ." Mrs. Fenway glanced at her wide-eyed son and then at Elspeth and closed her mouth.

"Good day to you, Mrs. Fenway, and thank you," Elspeth said with a smile.

"Good day, Miss Thompson."

Ezra followed her out of his mother's shop, holding the wrapped lace under his arm. "You needn't walk behind me, Ezra." She took the lace from his hands and put it in her bag along with the thread.

The young man hurried to walk beside her, keeping pace with her swift stride. Elspeth tilted her face to the sun, feeling its warmth, letting it seep into her muscles and make her feel as if all things she'd dreamed of were possible. That pleasurable feeling did not last long.

"Get your hands off me, you filthy copper," a woman shouted.

Elspeth looked up at the doorway of the bawdy house she was nearing. There was an older man, with mutton chops and a nearly bald head, being dragged out the door by a younger man in a dark suit. The woman who had shouted, the one in the chemise and red corset Elspeth had seen earlier, was hanging on to the bald man's sleeve, trying to drag him back inside the brick row house. There were no policemen in sight, but a crowd had gathered, mostly consisting of the young men who'd taunted Elspeth on her walk to Mrs. Fenway's.

"'E ain't going nowheres until 'e 'ands over me fee," she screamed and yanked on the bald man's jacket. Elspeth heard a ripping sound. The woman reached around the bald man and kicked at the younger man with a pointy-toed shoe.

"Ouch," he said and rubbed his thigh with his loose hand. "Let go of him, and I'll pay you."

The woman spit at the younger man, and the bald one found his footing and cuffed the woman hard across the face. She crumbled to the stoop with a cry, holding her face in her hands.

"Fucking whore telling me what to pay," the red-faced bald man shouted to cheers from the crowd of popinjays.

The woman looked up from where she cowered, and Elspeth could see blood running from her nose and lip. She'd seen enough.

"Stop!" she shouted as she picked up her skirts and hurried up the steps. "Stop this instant!"

Elspeth crouched down and pulled a handkerchief from her drawstring bag. She handed it to the woman, who looked up at her guardedly. Elspeth leaned forward and dabbed the blood from the woman's chin and mouth while the young men on the street in front of the house continued their taunts. She stood quickly and turned to the bald man.

"Pay her! Pay her this minute," she said.

The young man stepped between them. "There's no reason for you to get involved, miss. Please be on your way."

She batted his hand away when he reached for her. "Don't you dare touch me! You and your . . . your father are here together? How disgusting you are!"

The crowd roared their approval, and she could see Mrs. Fenway and Ezra at the edge of the crowd. The shop owner said something to her son, and he raced down the street, away from his mother's shop.

"This is not my . . ." the young man said, clearly affronted.

"Then why are you here with him? What need do you have to frequent this house?"

The young man's mouth twitched, and that was when she noticed he was startlingly handsome. Strikingly so. The crowd on the street was taunting him, asking him to tell her about his need. She felt her face go red and wished she could have taken back her words, but it was too late. She would have to brazen it out and was about to repeat her question when the bald man leaned close to her.

"What do you know of this house, girl? Are you looking to audition? I'll be happy to recommend you if you meet my expectations." He let his eyes drift down to her bosom and farther still.

Elspeth stared at the bald man, three times her size, covered in the finest herringbone wool—yards of it, she estimated—his purple four-in-hand held in place with a glittering diamond stick pin. She did not retreat, not one inch, but held completely still, her eyes riveted on his. She would not be the one to look away. He turned suddenly and swept his hand in a wide arc.

"I think she likes me! I think she's fallen under my spell! And she'll like my long, fat sausage too, won't she, boys?" He turned to look at her, bending his knees just a bit to grab his crotch and thrust his hips at her. The men in the crowd roared their approval.

The young man was pulling on his arm. "Schmitt! That's enough. Come away."

Elspeth speared him with her glare. "Make an escape now after your da's had his way and not paid her and hit her too? Coward!"

The muscles in the young man's neck stood out white against the red color of his face and throat. He leaned around the bald man. "He is *not* my father, miss. You should go before you are caught up in something ugly. Go."

"As if this is not ugly enough, a grown man in a fine suit hitting a woman on the stoop of her home!"

"It could get worse. Go!" he growled as the crowd shouted their appreciation at whatever crude comments Schmitt had just made.

"I'll see her—" Elspeth began and stopped abruptly as her brother James shouldered past Schmitt and the young red-faced man. He put his hand under her arm, none too lightly, and turned her to go down the steps. Schmitt stepped in front of them.

"I saw her first, boy," he said. "Go on about your business."

"Come along, Elspeth," James said quietly without a glance at Schmitt.

"I'm sorry, miss," the young man said and reached out his hand as if hoping to shake hers. "Mr. Schmitt lost his head for a moment."

James leaned in and spoke quietly. "Don't touch my sister. Ever. And tell your friend to back out of our way."

"Or what, boy?" Schmitt asked and turned with a broad smile and a sweep of his arm to the crowd. "Or what?"

But other than a few whispered words and quick exchanges of coins, the young men crowded in the street were completely silent. They were all, as one, staring at her brother, clearly waiting for his response.

"You don't want to know," James said to Schmitt and turned his head to her. "Aunt Murdoch is worried about you."

"I highly doubt that," she said but held tight to her spot on the stoop. "This man has not paid this woman, and he hit her, James. It's not right."

"Unfortunately, she's in a business that is often dangerous. But we can do nothing for her. We're going, Elspeth."

The young man held out several paper bills. "Here. Give this to her, and then go before someone else is hurt."

Elspeth took the money and handed it to woman, still sitting on the doorway threshold, her hankie in the other woman's hand. The woman tried to return the hankie, now bloodstained, but Elspeth shook her head and smiled. "Do you have something for that?"

"Come on, Mary," a woman in a gauzy robe standing just inside the door said. "Come to the kitchen. We'll get some ice on it."

Mary stood on shaky legs and let the woman inside help her

until the door was closed. Elspeth turned to James. "We should be going," she said.

"Should we? You will be the death of me, Lizzie," James said with a quirk of his lips, using the childhood name that he knew she disliked.

They began down the steps together, and the boisterous men gathered around her and James as they finally skirted Schmitt, asking her brother all manner of questions, patting him on the back, and tugging on the brims of their caps to her or nodding in her direction. Elspeth glanced back at the young man, now watching her every movement. It was as if he was memorizing her features for some future inspection, and it made a chill run down her spine.

EXCERPT FROM INTO THE EVERMORE

Into the Evermore

November 1842 Virginia

"Twenty dollars and you can have her. Don't make no never mind to me what you do with her. I just want to see the gold first."

The filthy-looking bearded man waved his gun in every direction as he spoke, including at the head of the young woman he held in his arms and at the three men in front of him. The trio all had handkerchiefs covering the lower part of their faces and hats pulled down tight, revealing six eyes now riveted to the pistol as it honed in on one random target after the other. The woman was struggling, although it was a pitiful attempt as she was clearly exhausted, and maybe hurt. The wind whipped through the trees, blowing the dry snow in circles around them. Beau Gentry watched the grim scene play out as he peered around a boulder down into a small ravine. He'd been propped against the sheltered rock, dozing, and thinking he'd best start a fire, when he heard voices below.

EXCERPT FROM INTO THE EVERMORE

"Ain't paying twenty dollars in gold for some used-up whore," one of the masked men said.

The filthy man wrenched his arm tighter around the woman and put the gun to her temple. "Tell 'em, girly. Tell 'em you ain't no whore."

She shrank away from the barrel of the gun and moaned. "Please, mister. Let me go," she begged.

"Tell 'em you ain't no whore!"

She shook her head and pulled at the filthy man's arm around her waist. "I'm no fallen lady," she whispered. "I'm just, I'm just . . ." The woman went limp, and Beau thought she'd fainted but instead she vomited into the snow in front of her. He watched her choke and gag, bent over the man's arm, and that's when he realized she was barefoot.

Beau leaned back against the rock and checked his pistols and shotgun beside him. He hoped his horse wouldn't bolt from the tree she was loosely tied to when the bullets started to fly. It'd be a long walk back to Winchester if she did, especially as he'd most likely be carrying the woman. "Shit," he muttered. "Shit and damnation. She doesn't have any goddamn shoes on."

From his angle, he'd need to drop the three bandits with the two shells from the shotgun, and finish off any of them still breathing with one of his pistols. They'd be surprised and hopefully slow if the liquor smell floating on the wind meant anything. He was counting on the filthy man being hampered by the woman's struggling. He was hoping she didn't get shot in the cross fire, but then she'd be better off dead than facing what was in store for her if the filthy man was the victor. The argument over the gold was getting heated, he could hear, making this as good a time as any.

The snow fell away from the fur collar and trim of Beau's coat as he stood, lifted the shotgun to his shoulder, and aimed at the first man. He pulled the trigger, sighted in the second man, and pulled the second trigger right after the other, marching forward

EXCERPT FROM INTO THE EVERMORE

through brush and snow, letting the shotgun fall from his hands as he went. Two of the men dropped and the third fell to his knees, aiming his pistol at Beau as he did. Beau lengthened his stride, pulled a pistol from his waistband as he made the clearing, raised his left arm straight, and dropped the kneeling man to the ground with a shot to his face, letting the spent weapon fall to the ground. As he turned, he pulled his new fighting knife free of its scabbard and brought his right hand up, wielding a second pistol, side-stepping to get an angle on the filthy man.

"She's mine! You ain't getting her."

"Drop the gun."

"Twenty dollars in gold and you can have her!"

He wondered how much longer the woman would last. She was white-faced, except for the dirt, and her hair hung in clumps, matted together with blood. Her mouth was open in a silent scream. She raised and lowered her arms as if paddling in a pool of water. Most likely she was long past terrified and all the way to hysterical.

"Fine," Beau said. "You want twenty dollars?"

The filthy man nodded, and Beau dropped his knife in the snow and reached his hand in his pants pocket as if intending to retrieve a gold piece. The man lowered his weapon by an inch or so as his eyes followed Beau's hand, and in that moment Beau brought up his right hand and fired his weapon. The bullet tore through the man's neck, sending blood gushing into the snow as the man tumbled sideways, releasing the woman. She fell in the opposite direction, covered in splattered blood, clawing and crawling away from her captor, turning on her back and shoving off in the mud and snow with bleeding feet, pushing herself away. Her cry echoed in the silent cold night.

Beau pulled his knife from the snow, kicked away the filthy man's gun, and walked to where he lay, now writhing as he slowly drowned in his own blood. The hair on the back of Beau's neck stood and he turned. The last of the three men, missing part of his cheek and ear, had retrieved a loaded pistol from the belt of one of his companions and was now aiming it at Beau with shaking hands. Beau released the knife with a whip of his wrist, landing it dead center on the man's chest. He turned to the woman and watched as her eyes rolled back in her head and she crumbled the last four or five inches, until her back hit the forest floor.

LA
5/25

Made in the USA
Columbia, SC
29 June 2024